# RUN FAR, RUN FAST

*Other Avon Camelot books by* **WALT MOREY**

| | | |
|---|---|---|
| GENTLE BEN | 30155 | $1.25 |

# RUN FAR, RUN FAST

Walt Morey

Designed by *Nancy Danahy*

AVON BOOKS
A division of
The Hearst Corporation
959 Eighth Avenue
New York, New York 10019


Published by arrangement with E.P. Dutton and Company, Inc.
Library of Congress Catalog Card Number: 74-4228
ISBN: 0-380-43356-7



First Camelot Printing, May, 1979

*For the two Arthur Moreys who were*
*always on the sidelines cheering—*
*my father and my brother*

Nick Lyons stared out the kitchen window numb with grief. Harold and Alice Thompson's words came through the closed door like the voices of doom. With the funeral over, they were discussing what to do with him as if he were a piece of old furniture or a dog or cat to be disposed of.

"Now that his mother's gone Nick has no place to go. No one to care for him. We can manage with one more," Alice reasoned.

"We've got three. That's all I can support," Harold insisted. "We helped Elsie and Nick like good neighbors should. Now we've got to stop. Elsie's gone. I'm sorry for Nick, too. But there's nothing more we can do. My family comes first."

Two floors below a black sedan stopped at the curb. A woman got out and crossed the snow-packed street to the apartment house.

Harold's next words jerked the boy out of his grief.

"I've talked to the welfare people. Nick's their problem now. There should be somebody here to get him any time."

It would take the welfare woman about a minute to climb the stairs and find this apartment. He had to get out fast.

The fire escape came down outside the kitchen window. He climbed onto the sink and eased the window open. The knock came on the apartment door as he slipped through onto the fire escape.

Nick risked the icy steps two at a time. He was halfway down when Harold's voice yelled from the kitchen window above, "Nick! Come back here! Nick!"

Nick hit the lower landing, dropped through to the snowy street, and sprinted around the corner into the alley.

The alley was an old friend. It was littered with garbage cans, empty cartons, and boxes of all kinds. Every ancient building had its recessed windows, doorways, and stairwells to hide in. Nick raced two blocks and pressed himself into a darkened doorway.

In a couple of minutes the black sedan stopped at the mouth of the alley. Harold Thompson got out and crunched through the snow toward him. The woman stayed in the car. Nick pressed deeper into the shadowed recess, muscles tensed to leap and run. He doubted he could outrun Harold. Harold had long, powerful-looking legs. He'd once played football.

The crunching steps grew louder. Nick could hear the tiny squeak of slipping snow beneath Harold's feet.

A couple of more steps and he'd have no choice. The muscles of his legs began to tremble. He drew a careful breath and held it. He pressed his palms flat against the cold wall behind him to give himself a flying start.

The footsteps stopped. He was discovered! He waited for Harold's gruff command, "Come on out, Nick."

Silence tore at his nerves. In another second he'd have to leap and run or explode. Then the footsteps began again. They were going away. The car door slammed. The motor started. Nick let out his breath.

He remained in the dark doorway. He knew the routine. Several minutes later the black sedan slowly passed the mouth of the alley. A minute later it appeared at the opposite end. When it left this time Nick stepped out. The welfare woman and Harold would cruise up and down the streets trying to find him. If they failed, the woman would leave. But she'd return to the apartment at unexpected times and wait.

Nick wanted to go to the apartment for his overcoat, cap, mittens, and the few dollars in the cup on the shelf. But he didn't dare risk it. He might starve. He might even freeze to death without proper clothing. But anything was better than going to a home for orphans. Starting now he meant to get as far away from this city as possible.

He tried to plan a way to leave. Hiking was no good in these clothes and this weather. He thought of hitching rides but the first cop who saw him standing beside the road would pick him up.

Then he remembered the railroad yard. He'd seen

the long lines of freights coming and going, tramps riding the cars. There were no police there and the inside of a boxcar would be protection from the weather.

Nick headed for the yard eight blocks away. He kept to the alleys, appearing only briefly at the end of every block. Each time he stopped at the mouth of the alley and studied the street. When it was clear he dashed across. Once he thought he glimpsed the black sedan turning a corner far down the street.

The third cross street was the main drag of this old rundown section. He stood in the shelter of the alley and tightness gripped his throat. For all its scarred, neglected look, this had been his home for more than sixteen years. He'd played touch football and baseball here, dodging cars and trucks. His mother walked this street every day going to and from work. There wasn't a cat, dog, kid, or hiding place for escape from the tough South Side Gang he didn't know.

The street was clear. He sprinted across.

The railroad yard was a spider-web of tracks. Diesel engines shunted cars about. Hundreds of boxcars stood in waiting lines. Several trains were creeping out of the yard.

Nick huddled in the shelter of a small shed and waited. He wanted a train heading south, away from this winter cold. But there were few trains leaving.

It turned colder. The wind picked up. Fine snow began swirling and drifting. He turned up the collar of his suit coat and huddled, shivering. The light went out of the day. Dusk lay over the yard. A short freight pulled away, heading south. Nick ran alongside and tried to pry open a door. But he didn't know how, or else the door was stuck.

He was about to give up and head uptown for the night, where he knew a place to get warm, when a long freight approached. He scanned each car as it passed under the yard light. Finally he spotted an open door. Now that the train was approaching he was afraid his muscles had become so stiff with cold he couldn't catch it.

The car came opposite. He jumped out and began to run. His legs felt numb. He slipped and almost fell. Then the blood began to pump fiercely. He drew alongside the train. There was no handhold, no step. The train was gathering speed. He was going to lose it. In desperation he dove headfirst into the dark interior on his stomach. He landed half in and half out.

The floor was smooth. Nick began to slide backward, pulled by the weight of his dangling legs. He clawed frantically to stop himself. His legs were being sucked toward the turning wheels. He was going to fall! Then powerful hands clamped on his shoulders and he was lifted bodily inside. A gruff voice said, "Boy! you tryin' to get yourself killed?"

Nick twisted from the hands and backed against the wall. "I can take care of myself."

"Sure! Like you just did."

Nick could barely make out the solid bulk of a man in the dark. "I'd have got in," he insisted.

The man grunted. He closed the door to about a foot opening, then went into the heavy dark at the back of the car and sat down. Nick wanted to get away from the wind that knifed through the door opening, but he had to stay. If the man made a move toward him he could flop outside. He sat down in the full blast of the draft, keeping his ears tuned for any slight movement from the man.

The man's voice said, "You're gonna get cold there."

Nick didn't answer.

"I'm not interested in the few nickels in your pocket," the voice said. "Relax."

"I haven't any money."

"Sure you have. Every kid that runs away has a few bucks."

The train picked up speed. The clack-clack over the rail joints came faster. The flow of cold air increased. Nick moved a little farther from the door, but it didn't help. Numbness began creeping into him. He didn't know the man had left his place until his bulk loomed suddenly over him. Nick rolled away, scrambling wildly for the open door.

He was yanked to his feet and carried, kicking and fighting, into the black darkness of the car. There he was jammed down against the wall and the man grumbled, "Now stay put! You want pneumonia, go someplace else to get it. I don't figure to take care of you." The man sat down a few feet off and lapsed into silence.

Nick was out of the draft but he couldn't stop shivering. He wrapped his arms tight around himself to save the little heat in his body.

The man pulled off his heavy jacket and tossed it to Nick. "Put it on."

"I'm all right," Nick managed.

"Quit lyin'! Take off that soaked coat, spread it on the floor to dry, and get into the jacket."

The jacket was sizes too big, but it was heavy and warm from the man's body. Warmth began to spread through Nick, bringing delicious drowsiness. He concentrated on staying awake, but the rhythmic clacking of the wheels dragged him downward into sleep.

Gray dawn was lighting the inside of the car when Nick awoke. The man stood by the open door staring out at the passing country. He wore a thick woolen shirt, woolen pants, and heavy shoes. He turned and Nick got his first good look. The man was six or seven inches taller than Nick's five-and-a-half lean feet. There was a rock-hard massiveness in the breadth of his chest and shoulders. He wore no hat. His bullet head was completely bald. His face was broad, heavy-boned, and topped by thick red brows. He was smiling and the smile got into his brown eyes. "Feelin' better?"

Nick knew he had nothing to fear from this man. "The coat sure helped," he said. But he didn't feel much better. He was ravenously hungry. He felt his own coat on the floor. It was dry. He slipped out of the man's jacket and put on his coat.

The man got into his jacket and stood watching Nick thoughtfully. "We'll be pulling into North Forks soon," he said. "They've got a big yard. Lots of freights. You can catch one goin' back and be home by night." Nick looked up, surprised.

"I've seen lots of runaway kids. Usually one night

aboard a cold freight car with an empty belly and home looks pretty good."

"I've got no home."

"Any kid wearin' a suit, white shirt, and tie has a home."

"I haven't."

The brown eyes studied him soberly. "You wanna talk about it?"

"I want to forget it."

"Before you do you'd better fill me in on why you're runnin' away. I don't want no trouble with the police."

"You won't have any."

"I'll decide that. Now give."

"What do you want to know?"

"Let's start with your name, and don't give me a phony."

"Lyons. Nick Lyons."

"You can call me Idaho, everybody does. Now, about this no home?"

Nick thought he'd spent his grief, that he was through with crying. But he had to swallow before words would come.

He was surprised how little there was to tell. His mother and he had lived in the same apartment all Nick's life. His father walked out when Nick was five or six. Nick hardly remembered him. The apartment wasn't much—a bedroom, kitchen, and small living room. Nick's mother clerked in a store downtown. She made barely enough for them to get by. Nick helped out running errands and cleaning up in stores after school. Two months ago his mother took sick. The funeral was yesterday.

Idaho nodded as he talked. "I get the picture. Now you figure you're on your own and can bum around the country."

"I won't go to one of those orphans' homes or whatever they call them."

"What about uncles and aunts?"

"Pa had a brother someplace. He wouldn't be interested. There's nobody else."

Idaho crossed his legs thoughtfully. "How old are you?"

"Almost seventeen."

"Still sixteen. About third-year high school?"

"Yes."

"Funny. You and I started out almost the same way."

"How?"

"I ran away at fourteen. Been ridin' the rods ever since."

"You're a bum?"

"That's one name." Idaho smiled. "There's also hobo, tramp, bo, or bohunk, and knight-of-the-road. Personally I like knight-of-the-road. Sounds more romantic. Fact is, I consider myself a free soul."

"How do you mean?"

"I answer to no job or clock. I work when I want to. I go wherever I fancy, and mostly the railroad takes me there. North in summer, south in winter. I migrate with the ducks and geese."

"It sounds great."

Idaho looked down at him, smiling faintly. "It's no good."

"But you said. . . ."

"I know what I said. It's no good. Man should light

someplace, put down roots, have a home and friends he can gab with over the back fence. There's more to livin' than watching the world go by an open boxcar door."

"If you don't like it, why do you do it?"

"It's a way of life, all I know. You learn to like it after a fashion." Idaho leaned his head against the wall, brown eyes thoughtful. "At first it's kind of fun. Just goin' and goin', seein' the country. You tell yourself when you find that certain spot you'll light. Somehow you never find it. There's always something wrong. The next place will be better. Finally, if you're honest, you admit you've been at it too long. You can't quit. You live to learn what's around the next corner, over the next hill, to see what exciting, wonderful thing will happen to you tomorrow. Mostly nothing does."

The train began slowing down. "We'll be pulling into the yard soon. You can still go back."

"To an orphans' home with a bunch of other kids? No, sir!" Nick said emphatically.

"How far do you figure to run to keep ahead of the authorities?"

"As far as I have to," Nick said.

"I mighta known," Idaho mused on a note of disgust. "About once a year I wind up playin' nurse to some wet-nosed kid that's not dry behind the ears."

"I can look out for myself," Nick said stiffly.

"Do tell," Idaho said sarcastically. "Why, in a week you'd starve, or freeze, or get run over. Or maybe beat to death in some hobo jungle. You don't even know how to get aboard a moving train."

Nick said nothing.

"I'm trying to give you the picture, boy," Idaho said. "Once you start ridin' the rods you'll never have a home and family, few friends, if any. And nobody'll care if you live or die."

"Nobody cares now," Nick said.

Idaho's brown eyes studied him a moment. "You'd better be sure of that. Dead certain sure."

"I am."

Idaho looked out the open door at the passing landscape. "Well," he said finally, "that's settled. Now, you need some different clothes. You got any money at all?"

Nick shook his head. "I didn't have time to grab what little there was."

"We'll manage," Idaho said. "I've got enough to feed us until we can find a job or two of work."

"Keep track of what you spend on me," Nick said. "I'll pay you back."

"We're gonna get along just fine." Idaho smiled and thrust out a big hand. "Welcome to the Knights-of-the-Road, partner."

# 2 

"Now then," Idaho said in a business-like voice, "the first thing you've got to learn is how and when to get into and out of a boxcar. You picked the wrong time and place last night. You were at the edge of the yard where the train was picking up speed. You've got to be inside where it's going slow. When there's no handhold to help you in, you jump and turn so you land sitting down and facing out. Never dive in head first. You could smash your head on some cargo or be sucked out, as you almost were."

"I'll do whatever you say," Nick said.

"Good. Another thing I especially want to impress on you. When you've got cash money never flash it around. Never admit you've got any. We may all be Knights-of-the-Road but there's some that'll knock you in the head for a nickel."

The train's speed dropped off fast. Idaho stood up. "Come on, we're due to leave this private luxury coach in a few minutes."

They stood in the open door while the freight crawled into the yard and stopped. Nick started to jump to the ground but Idaho held him back. "Never jump without lookin' first. A boxcar could be runnin' free on this track alongside—or another train coming. You can't always hear 'em with all the other racket. Always look first. Okay! All clear. Go ahead."

Fine snow covered the ground. A biting wind picked it up and swirled it across the freight yard. Cold knifed through Nick's thin suit.

Idaho said, "First thing is to get you some clothes. Come on, I know a place."

"How'll I get clothes without money?"

"I'll show you. We're going to a place called The Lighthouse."

Nick fell in beside him. "We going to steal 'em?"

"I never steal."

"Then how?"

"Just watch. You'll learn."

They hiked six frigid blocks and turned into an old store building whose dusty windows were packed with an assortment of used clothing. Inside row on row of clothing hung on racks. Halfway down an aisle a tall, lean old man with a great shock of white hair and a full beard bore down on them. "Idaho! Odaho!" he boomed. "As I live and breathe! I'd about give up on you this year. You know what that white stuff is flyin' around out there?"

"Too cold for sugar," Idaho said.

"Right you are. How come you're two months late?"

"I was detained," Idaho said. They shook hands.

The old man's blue eyes studied Idaho. "Was you, by chance, in somebody's stony lonesome?"

"I need somethin' for my noggin'," Idaho said. "You got some warm caps?"

"You was in somebody's stony lonesome. Caps and hats're right here. Find your fit.

"Did you rob a bank or beat up on somebody or was you standin' on th' wrong street corner at th' right time?"

Idaho was pawing through a pile of caps and hats. "Nick," he said, "this's Cap Small. Don't ask what he was captain of, a rowboat most likely if anything."

Cap Small's hand was big and hard. His knowing blue eyes kept studying Idaho. He nodded his head wisely. "You was standin' on th' wrong street corner," he said positively. "Idaho, I'm surprised."

"I'll take this cap," Idaho said. "Nick's travelin' with me. He needs to trade in these fancy duds for some decent clothes. You know. Wool pants, shirt, jacket, heavy shoes."

"Trade!" Cap Small almost shouted. "I'm in th' business of sellin'. Can't you get that through your bald head?"

"You trade me."

"You're always broke—so you say. Anyway, you're a special case."

"So's Nick. He's my partner."

"They're always your partner."

They both sounded angry. But Nick could see they had trouble not smiling. They were friends, glad to see each other. This was their greeting.

"Well, all right. Just this once more." Cap Small headed for the back of the store grumbling. "You'll bust me yet. Every time you come in it takes a whole day's profit to make it up."

"Come off it," Idaho said, "I know better'n that. We're tradin' you a practically new suit in good shape, white shirt, tie, good oxfords. All for some old rough duds you probably got for nothin'."

"You ever think of goin' into th' clothing business?" Cap Small grumbled.

"Too confining," Idaho answered promptly.

Twenty minutes later Nick was outfitted in heavy shoes, woolen pants, shirt, jacket, and cap. Cap Small watched them leave. "I s'pose I'll have th' bad luck to see you next year."

Idaho nodded. "I always save you my business."

"Don't do me so many favors," Cap Small said. "A few more like this and I'll be on th' street with a tin cup."

"If you are," Idaho said, "the cup'll be big as a barrel and jam-packed with money. So long."

"Did he lose money on us?" Nick asked when they were outside.

"Naw. But he wouldn't be happy not bellyachin'. We've been jawin' each other for years. Great man, Cap. What say we eat?"

They turned into a small restaurant and sat at the counter. Idaho said to the waitress, "Two stacks of hotcakes, bacon, and eggs. Coffee for me, milk for him."

"I drink coffee," Nick said.

"Not with me. Milk's got more nourishment. You need twenty pounds on you."

While they waited Nick asked, "Idaho's not your real name?"

Idaho smiled, "If you said Peter Jamieson nobody'd know who you meant."

"How'd you get the name?"

"A long time ago somebody asked me where I was from. They called me Idaho Red when I had hair Been just Idaho a long time."

Their breakfasts came. They ate hungrily.

Back in the yard they caught a freight. Inside an empty car they sat side by side. Nick felt comfortable, relaxed. His stomach was full, he was warm, and Idaho had taken over. He said, "You knew a freight would be pulling out heading south."

Idaho nodded. "It's one of the things you learn. We'll ride this one all day, maybe all night. Then we'll get off, eat, and catch another. Today, tonight, tomorrow, and tomorrow night should put us in a warmer climate. Then we'll stop a few days, get work, and build up our bank accounts."

"You know where we can get jobs?"

"I know a thousand places."

Nick thought about that. "You must know a lot."

"You get to be a jack of a lotta trades. You don't master any."

Nick remembered something and asked, "What's a stony lonesome?"

"A jail." Idaho smiled.

He didn't want to ask but he had to. "Were you in one?"

Idaho shook his head. "A barn burned. I stayed longer than usual to help a rancher build a new one."

"How come you let Cap Small think you'd been in jail?"

"It made him feel good."

Nick lapsed into thoughtful silence. The clack-

clack over the rail joints came faster. "Idaho," he asked, "why are you bothering with me?"

"Company's nice. I like good company."

"You could travel faster without me, and cheaper, because I'm broke. And I don't know a thing about jobs."

"You think someplace along the line there's a payoff?"

"Nobody does things for nothing."

"What do you figure the payoff with me will be?"

"That's what worries me. I haven't any money to pay."

"You've met some wrong people," Idaho said. "Everybody's not tryin' to shoot an angle. Now you take Cap Small. He sounds tough and he can be at times. But you'd be surprised at the people he's helped."

"He's got to get something," Nick insisted.

"Oh, he does. A good feelin' in here." Idaho tapped his chest.

"Alice and Harold's good feeling for helping Ma and me was getting our furniture," Nick said bitterly. "Pa's was walking out on us."

"There's people like that," Idaho agreed. "Mostly they're a sorry lot. Everybody needs a hand sometime. I've been helped plenty. So I help you. Somebody gets in a bind, you help them. You don't expect pay. You do it because you want to, because somebody helped you. Life's not all goin' around with your hand out, or tryin' to get the best of the other feller. It's giving, too; maybe only advice, or friendship, or a little encouragement."

"That wouldn't work where I came from," Nick

said emphatically. "Everybody there is out for number one."

"It takes all kinds to make a world," Idaho said mildly. "Maybe you'll be one of those, too. Time'll tell."

All day they rode through flat farmland and softly falling snow. With evening they entered the mountains. The freight began laboring upgrade. The cold increased. Idaho slid the door completely closed and they were in pitch dark. They leaned, shoulders together, and napped and listened to the rhythmic clacking of the wheels through the long night. At one point Idaho murmured, "Notice anything new?"

"No, what?"

"Clackin's getting faster. We're over The Divide and heading downhill. Getting over the hump always makes me feel better."

At noon they left the train in the rain in a small town, ate, and caught another freight two hours later. They rode until morning and dropped off in a large valley whose slopes were patterned with orchards. Idaho looked about and said, "Maybe we can get jobs winter pruning here."

"I don't know anything about pruning trees," Nick said. "I've never even seen an apple growing on a tree."

"You won't now. I'm about broke. Come on."

None of the big orchardists wanted Nick but Idaho said, "We're partners. He works or I don't." They needed Idaho so Nick worked, too.

"You were bluffing, weren't you?" Nick asked.

"Was I?" Idaho smiled.

"You might've lost the job."

"But I didn't."

They stayed a week and Idaho said Nick had a feel for pruning. When they left Nick had earned thirty dollars. He paid Idaho back and had ten dollars left. "Why don't we head for California," he said. "This ten'll pay my eats till we get there."

"Why California so fast?"

"That's where I was headed the night we met. Besides," Nick smiled, "it's warm there and I always liked oranges."

"It's still too far to make a straight run for it on this cash," Idaho said. "We'll get there in due time."

They continued across country, working a few days here, a week there. Idaho's vast experience was always in demand. No one wanted Nick. But Idaho insisted, "We're partners. He works or I don't."

Idaho always commanded top wages. Nick didn't. And there were expenses besides board and room on the job. Nick had to buy a pair of rubber boots for one job, then left them when they moved on. He wore out a pair of canvas gloves a day. He needed shirts, sweaters, pants. But the ten dollars slowly swelled to fifty, sixty. He asked Idaho what to do with it.

"When you get, say, a hundred, put it in a bank like I do. Then you have to remember where the bank is." He showed Nick a trick with his sixty dollars. He laid the bills flat between pieces of newspaper, then spread them carefully in the bottom of Nick's shoe. "Nobody'll guess you got it," he said.

In time they came to the Pacific Coast, into the

heart of the last great stands of virgin fir forests. Nick saw his first sawmill. They crossed a river where three big tugs strained at a raft of logs almost a mile long. They passed fleets of trucks loaded high with logs bound for the mills.

One night they waited beneath a trestle for a freight and Nick asked, "When are we heading flat-out for California?"

"Wanna see what's over the next hill and around the bend?"

"Some. Mostly I want to see oranges growing on a tree."

"Same thing. Your foot itchin'?"

"No."

"It will soon. Okay. We'll stay with this next freight all the way."

Two men slid down the bank and came under the trestle. One was big, with wide, thick shoulders. His pale eyes were close together, giving him an appearance of scowling. A half-smoked cigarette hung between his thick lips. The second was short, with heavy muscles overlayed with layers of fat. His eyes hit Nick and Idaho and slid away. They sat down a few feet off. The big man finished his cigarette. "You fellers headin' south?"

"Not sure," Idaho said.

"Of course we are." Nick was annoyed with Idaho. "We agreed. Remember?"

"If you don't hop this next freight you'll be stuck here thirty-six hours, maybe more," the big man said.

"How so?" Idaho asked.

"Wreck sixty, seventy miles back. Cars scattered all

over th' country. Couple hundred yards of track ripped up. One freight got through ahead of it. Th' one comin'."

"I guess we'll wait." Idaho made as if to rise.

"But this train's heading south," Nick insisted. "We'll have to wait almost two days for another." Now that his mind was made up Nick couldn't wait to get into the bright California sunshine.

"I think we'd better wait." Idaho's brown eyes were steady on Nick. "There's no rush. We can work a few days. Pick up a stake."

"We've got plenty of stake."

"I say wait."

Overhead the rails began to hum. Nick jumped up and began scrambling up the bank. "Here she comes! Here she comes!" Idaho and the two men followed.

They found a door ajar about halfway down the line of slow-moving cars and piled in. Nick and Idaho sat on one side, the two strangers on the other. Nick was jubilant. By the time the track was cleared they'd be at the California line.

The bills Nick carried in his right shoe had formed a hard lump under his instep. He unlaced his shoe, got a hand down inside, worked the bills flat again, and relaced the shoe. When he looked up the little man was watching. Nick saw him smile and close his eyes.

The train picked up speed. California, Nick thought, here I come. The oranges he'd seen on grocery counters he'd pick right off the tree and eat. How about that!

Darkness came. Nick began to get sleepy. The two

men across the car had been sleeping for some time. The big fellow lay flat on his back, hat pulled over his eyes. The little one sat hunched up, head on his pulled-up knees.

Idaho asked in a low voice, "You sleepy?"

"A little."

"Then get some sleep. I'll stay awake. When you wake up I'll sleep."

"You mean one of us should stay awake? Why?"

"Because I said so." Idaho's voice was sharp. "Okay?"

"Sure," Nick said. He slid down, turned up the collar of his jacket, and was soon asleep.

When Nick awoke he guessed it must be somewhere past the middle of the night. He could barely make out the two men across the car. It didn't look as though they'd moved. He sat up and shoved up his cap.

Idaho asked, "Think you can stay awake now?"

"Sure, but why . . . ?"

"Just stay awake. Anything happens give me a punch."

"Sure. I will."

Idaho slid down on his shoulder blades, put an arm across his eyes, and slept.

Nick sat in the dark listening to the clacking of the wheels and feeling the slight rocking of the car. He studied the shapes of the two men and wondered how they could sleep so long. He thought of Idaho's insistence that one of them stay awake. Of course it was because of these two men. They'd been in cars with a dozen others and no one bothered to stay awake.

Idaho was touchy today. Nick put his head back against the wall and yawned. The rhythmic clacking was like a lullaby. He began thinking of California and orange groves again.

Nick jerked his head up with a start. He had dropped off to sleep for a minute. Then he became aware that his right shoe was slowly being eased off his foot. He made out the black bulk of the short man kneeling before him. He kicked out with all his strength and yelled, "Idaho!" at the top of his lungs. His stocking foot slammed into a chest. The man fell over backward with a surprised grunt. Nick scrambled forward on all fours searching for his shoe. He was aware Idaho had lunged erect and was locked with the big man who'd charged out of nowhere. He found the shoe. Then he heard the big man yell frantically, "Shorty! Shorty, help me! Help. He's killin' me!"

The short, fat man's shadow rose from the floor where Nick had kicked him and leaped at the struggling men. The three went rocking, twisting, and crashing into the black depths of the car.

The big man's voice panted, "Get 'is arm. Get it, quick!" There were the sounds of falling bodies, of scramblings across the floor. Out of the dark came the sodden smash of fists on flesh, curses, cries of pain and rage. For a moment Nick froze. Then panic engulfed him. He threw himself frantically toward the open door and launched his body out into the night.

# 3

Nick was lost. It seemed he'd been hiking for hours up this narrow gravel road. He was ravenously hungry. He was tired, discouraged, a little frightened at the rugged immensity of the land. He was beginning to suspect this lonely, twisting road led nowhere. He hadn't seen a house, a car, or human for miles.

He felt he was somewhere in the center of a mysterious, primeval forest of giant trees. Moisture clung to the slender tips of fir needles. It glistened on tree trunks and barren limbs and soaked the rank undergrowth that blanketed the soggy earth. Fog tendrils ghosted high through the trees and hid the peaks of mountains that rose menacingly on all sides. Not a breath of air moved. No sound but that of his own feet broke the stillness.

Nick decided he'd hike around the next bend. If the road ahead looked no more promising than the miles behind he'd have to return to the small town he'd passed early this morning. The thought worried him. Any local lawman was sure to take notice of a strange boy and ask questions.

Around the bend the road was more of the same—except for one thing. A girl in the middle of it was struggling with an animal that Nick figured was a sheep. She was about fifteen. She wore jeans and a man's shirt. Her black, shiny hair hung loosely down her back. She had a rope around the animal's neck and was trying to pull it. The sheep had wicked curved horns and long, white wool. It stood head up, legs braced against the girl's pull.

"Darn you, George!" She yanked on the rope. "Move, you stubborn brute."

Nick said, "You're not taking that sheep anyplace if he don't want to go."

The girl seemed to become aware of him. "He's not a sheep. He's an Angora goat."

"Oh," Nick said.

She yanked on the rope again. "Well, don't just stand there!" she said annoyed. "Get behind and shove."

"Can he kick?"

"Of course. He's got legs, hasn't he? But he won't. Go on, what're you afraid of?"

Nick approached the rear of the goat. "What's his name?"

"George."

"Crazy name for a goat."

"He's a crazy goat. Go on. Shove!"

Nick pushed gingerly against the goat's rump. The girl pulled with all her strength. George gave a forward hop. The girl was overbalanced and fell. The next instant George dropped his head and lunged. Too late Nick opened his mouth to yell. George banged her from behind and drove her flat. He stood there shaking his horns menacingly, going "Ba-a-a-a."

The girl sat up and shook her fist. "Someday," she threatened, "you'll get a clubbing."

Nick tried not to laugh.

The girl scrambled up and handed him the rope. "You pull. I'll shove."

"Which way do you want to go?"

"Up the road."

Nick leaned into the rope and pulled with all his five-foot-seven and hundred thirty-five pounds. The goat was surprisingly strong. He didn't budge. Nick handed the rope to the girl, went to the edge of the road, broke off a switch, and stripped it. "Use this when I pull," he said.

They tried again. George braced. The girl cut him sharply with the whip and he jumped in surprise. Nick was overbalanced and fell. He'd just got to his knees when he was smashed a terrific wallop from behind. It drove him flat on his face. When he rolled over, the girl was squatting on her heels grinning. "You still think it's funny?"

George was glaring at them, shaking his horns menacingly again.

"He always do that?" Nick asked angrily.

"When you stoop over around George always face him."

"Why didn't you tell me?"

"I thought you'd like to find out for yourself."

Nick got up. "How far do you have to take him?"

"About half a mile."

"He going to be like this all the way?"

"Once he starts he'll go fine."

"Then let's start him."

This time Nick watched George as he yanked on the rope. The girl cut him across the hind legs. George jumped, ran past Nick, and began to pull.

They went up the road, George mincing along ahead of them, head up, looking importantly about, as if this was what he intended to do all along.

"Where you taking him?" Nick asked. "To the butcher, I hope."

"Home."

"He run away?"

"Ad Nelson drives his cows past our place to pasture morning and night. George goes up and stays with the cows all day. We've got cows, too, but he likes Ad's. At night when Ad takes his cows home, George usually stops at our place. Last night he didn't. This morning I had to go after him." She looked at Nick, her eyes big, brown, and curious. "I've never seen you before."

"No." To forestall further questions he asked, "You know anybody that can use some help for a few days?"

"You mean work?"

"Yes."

"Where you from?"

"Off a-ways." He waved vaguely.

"How come you're looking for work? Your folks here?"

"You always ask so many questions?" Nick asked annoyed.

"It's kind of queer you coming up this old logging road where there's only a couple of houses looking for work."

Nick had no answer to that. They walked in silence, George pulling ahead of them with an air of leading the way.

Finally they rounded a turn and came to an old house and cluster of outbuildings. The house was white and looked well kept. The outbuildings were red. They sat in a cleared space of about ten or twelve acres. George turned into the lane. Nick and the girl followed.

A tall, rawboned man with a shock of black hair came to meet them. He asked the girl, "Trouble, Connie?"

"That George . . ." the girl said. She indicated Nick. "He came along and helped."

The man held out a hand, "I'm Frank McCumber. This's my daughter, Connie, if she hasn't introduced herself."

Frank McCumber's hand was big, bony, and work-hard. Nick said, "I'm Nick Lyons. You know anybody that could use a few day's work?"

"I might. You alone?"

"Yes."

"Heading anyplace special?"

The question was asked casually but Nick felt the probing. This man had been around. He couldn't be fooled. "Yes," he said, "California."

"Broke?"

Nick nodded. "Broke."

"Hungry?" McCumber smiled.

"I could sure eat."

"Let's do that first. We can talk work afterward. Connie, turn George loose and come on."

Connie slipped the rope over the goat's head and he minced off toward the barn.

"That George!" McCumber smiled.

The kitchen was warm, mouth-watering with the aroma of cooked food. A tall, slender woman, sleeves rolled above brown forearms, was putting steaming dishes on a table. Nick guessed she was about forty-five.

McCumber said, "Norah, this is Nick Lyons. He helped Connie bring George home. He's going to have lunch with us. Then we'll discuss a little work."

"Hello, Nick." Norah McCumber's smile was quick and friendly. Nick revised his age guess downward to forty. "Thanks for helping Connie." She reached for another plate. "Hurry and wash. Lunch is ready."

Lunch was a banquet. There was a roast, potatoes, gravy, a stack of homemade bread, vegetables, and a pitcher of milk. They pushed food on Nick until he couldn't eat another bite.

Finally McCumber shoved back his chair. "You ever do any logging, Nick?"

"You mean cutting down big trees?"

"You haven't."

"We didn't have trees like these where I lived."

"Where was that?" Norah McCumber asked.

"Chicago."

Her blue eyes studied him. "It's most unusual a boy your age wandering this almost deserted logging road looking for work."

"I told him that," Connie piped up.

"Where are your parents?" she asked. "Are you running from the police or somebody? We could get into trouble hiring you if you are."

Caution raced through Nick. Then he reminded himself these people were not the law. They'd fed him. They didn't look or act dangerous. There was a chance to earn desperately needed money. Lastly he was sitting at the end of the table nearest the door. McCumber would have to come around the table to block his escape. The moment the man moved Nick could jump and run. Within half a minute he could lose himself in the trees. He said carefully, "The police may be after me, but not like you think. I didn't kill or rob anybody and I didn't escape from anyplace."

"Do you want to tell us about it?" McCumber asked.

Nick hesitated.

"Maybe we can help," Norah McCumber offered.

"What do you want to know?"

"Anything. The more we know the better we can understand."

"I lived in Chicago with my mother," he began, "not on the best side of the city." The memory was as sharp as ever but the time with Idaho had dulled the edge of pain.

It took longer to tell of his weeks with Idaho than it did his whole life before.

"But for Idaho I'd have died," Nick finished. "He bought clothes, fed me, took care of me like . . . like a father. He taught me what I had to know to ride the rods."

"He was a tramp." Connie's voice was sharp, her mouth tight.

"That's one name. There's bum, hobo, bohunk, knight-of-the-road. Idaho liked knight-of-the-road."

"He sounds like quite a person," McCumber said. "Where is he now?"

Nick told them about the freight train, the fight in the black-dark of the car. "I should've helped Idaho. But I panicked. I jumped out of the boxcar and ran."

"Not much else you could do," McCumber said. "Three men fighting in the dark is no place for a boy."

"He was my friend. I should have stayed. Maybe it would have made a difference. I hope he didn't get hurt."

"From what you've said this Idaho must be quite a man," McCumber said. "In the dark I'll bet he did all right taking care of himself. I wouldn't worry about it."

"How did you happen to come up this old logging road instead of catching another freight?" Norah McCumber asked. "A half dozen freights pass through Jewel daily."

"There was a wreck some miles back. Ours was the last train through. It would take a couple of days to repair the tracks. I couldn't hang around a little town. The local law would spot a strange kid sure. They're not putting me in one of those orphans' homes. Nobody's stopping me from getting to California."

"Why California?" she asked.

"It was snowing in Chicago. All I could think of was getting away to sunshine. Besides, I hear the big farm owners there don't ask too many questions about who you are."

"You plan to work on some farm?" McCumber asked.

"Until I'm eighteen and the police can't bother me."

"Then what?"

Nick shook his head. "I'll wait till I'm eighteen."

"Now you need a job to earn money to take you south," McCumber said.

"Yes."

"I've got a one-man logging operation here. I can use some help for a few days. It wouldn't take long to make a hook-tender of you. I can pay sixty cents an hour, give you a place to sleep and all you can eat. Interested?"

Before Nick could answer, Norah McCumber said, "He can do it. Allen did. They're about the same age and size." She bit her lip. "He . . . he even looks a little like Allen."

Connie said sharply, "You can't compare him to Allen. And I don't think Dad should hire him."

"Why?" McCumber asked.

Her cheeks were red. "He's a bum, a tramp. They're no good. They steal and lie." Her voice dropped and her eyes became big. "They—they even murder people."

"That was a year ago," her father pointed out.

"But it happened. It happened. He walked right past me. He looked right at me." Her voice was climbing.

"A one time in a million tragedy," McCumber said. "You can't condemn a lot of people for what one did. Besides, Nick's no tramp or bum. He's a young man going someplace, California. He's had more than his share of trouble. Don't you add to it."

Connie bit her lip and said nothing.

McCumber looked at Nick. "You interested in working with me?"

"Yes," Nick said.

"Good." McCumber glanced at his wife. "Nick can sleep in Allen's old room."

Norah McCumber said quickly, "I—I'll fix a bed out in the shed."

Frank McCumber seemed about to say something, then he pushed back his chair. "If I'm going to make a hook-tender of you let's get going."

They stopped on the porch and McCumber changed his house slippers for a pair of calked boots. From there they went to a shed about fifty feet from the house. The open front was filled with wood blocks and a chopping ax. The room was in back. It was bare, with one small window and an unmade bunk. It smelled damp.

Frank McCumber said, "We've got a good mattress and plenty of blankets. It'll look respectable when Norah gets through with it." He sat on the bunk. "About that room in the house—it was Allen's, our son's. He was killed by a rolling log last fall. He was about your age, your size. He looked a lot like you.

Norah and Connie haven't got over his loss yet." He rubbed his chin. "Neither have I. I'm just taking it better."

"This's fine," Nick said. "I've slept in boxcars and under bridges. What about a tramp murdering somebody?"

"The Grahams were an elderly couple who lived up the road about half a mile. Last year this tramp stopped and they hired him to work around the place. He murdered them one morning and took off. Connie was coming past the house from picking blackberries and he walked by her and went down the road. Later they figured he'd just committed the murders. It got Connie. She can hardly pass the house."

"Did they catch him?"

McCumber nodded. "Connie had to identify him. I'm sorry she included you with that kind of character."

"I can stand it."

"Good."

They went out and took a dirt road past the outbuildings and into the deep shadows of the big trees. McCumber talked as they wound among the giant trees. "We've got two hundred acres here. An uncle homesteaded it years ago. He willed it to me. We've been here three years. We've got a couple of hundred chickens and two cows. They just about take care of our day-to-day expenses. I started logging last fall."

A half mile later they came to a partially cleared spot where there was a small old caterpillar tractor with a blade. A number of medium-sized trees had been felled and cut into logs about forty feet long.

"We'll haul these to the river with the 'cat,' " Mr. McCumber explained, "make up a raft and I'll call the mill. They'll send their tug for them."

McCumber started the "cat" and showed Nick how to hook the cable around the log. Then with Nick following he pulled it to the river bank. Nick unhooked it, and under the man's instructions went down the bank to the water's edge with a twelve-foot pike pole, a spear-like pole with a needle-sharp point.

"Be sure to stand clear," Mr. McCumber warned. "When the log hits the water hold it close to the bank with the pike pole. The current's strong. It could suck the log out to the middle of the river and we'd lose it."

Nick watched the "cat" roll the log to the lip of the bank. There it came alive and bounced down the bank. The log hit the river with a mighty splash. Nick rushed in, drove the point of the pike pole into the middle of the log, and held on. He hadn't realized the tremendous strength of the river. Step by step it dragged him into the water, to his knees, then halfway to his hips.

Frank McCumber ran down the bank with another pike pole, slammed it into the end of the log, and shouted, "Take your point out."

Nick twisted free and waded ashore. The man held the end of the log close and let the current swing it in a half circle. When it came close to shore he steered it downstream into a small backwater where a dozen other logs were held by a cable.

Nick learned to spear the end of the log and do the same thing Frank McCumber did. He experienced no more trouble. He pulled and hauled on the heavy cable until his arms were numb. A knife-sharp ache settled under his shoulder blades. He had trouble turning the hook so it would hold. It came loose again and again. But Frank McCumber had infinite patience. "You'll get it," he encouraged. "It takes a little time. Don't hurry."

Once the cable slipped. The hook shot past Nick's head like a bullet. "Stand clear once it's hooked," McCumber warned. "That could kill you."

Nick had no gloves. His hands were torn by jaggers, tiny broken strands of cable. Frank McCumber noticed they were bleeding and gave him his gloves. "Why didn't you yell?" he scolded.

When they finally quit for the day Nick was bone tired and ravenously hungry. They'd put four more logs in the backwater.

McCumber slapped him on the back, "You're a good hook-tender. Tired?"

Nick nodded, "It's harder than it looks." He leaned against the "cat" sizing up one of the logs. "I'll bet they make a racket when they fall."

"You'll see before you leave. Let's go home."

They took the "cat" in to service it. Nick rode the drawbar.

Supper was on the table. Nick was trying to wash his torn palms when Norah McCumber saw them. She got a bottle of disinfectant and doctored the cuts. "Why did *you* let him go out there without gloves?" she demanded.

"I didn't think," McCumber said. "He'll have 'em tomorrow."

Again Nick ate until he was stuffed. Afterward

they did chores. Connie gathered eggs, fed the chickens, and put George into a small stanchion in the barn and fed him goat pellets. McCumber let in the two cows, Blackie and Fawn, and fed and milked them. The milk was then poured into metal cans and set by the road for the truck to pick up in the morning.

It was the first evening Nick had ever spent before a crackling fireplace. McCumber settled down with a local paper. Norah McCumber patched a shirt and Connie sat at the table scowling over school books. She kept stealing looks at Nick, brown eyes troubled, her lips tight.

Nick didn't know he had dozed until Norah McCumber said, "Nick, why don't you turn in?"

Frank McCumber went to the shed with him.

The bunk was made up. A chair was added. Curtains covered the window. A globe had been put in the drop cord.

"Hope it's all right," McCumber said.

"It's fine." Nick sat on the bunk. It was soft. There were a lot of covers.

McCumber said, "Sleep in tomorrow if you like. It's Sunday." About to leave, he said thoughtfully, "Odd set of incidents, wasn't it?"

"How do you mean?"

"The train wreck that stopped all traffic, the fight in the car, you coming up this road, stopping here, and looking so much like Allen. Sort of like it was meant to be." He smiled. "I'm kind of a fatalist. Believe things happen for a reason. Wonder what this one could be? I'm glad you stopped, Nick."

Nick watched him go up the lane and enter the

house. The cold night air had knocked the sleep out of him. He watched dusk come down off the high ridges and lay softly over the valley. The stars came out. A thin moon rode over the tree tops. An owl talked and was answered from deep in the woods. Chickens complained drowsily. George strutted from the barn and began nibbling at a bush.

This was a long way from the orange groves and sunshine of California. But it wasn't the snow of Chicago either. He thought of Idaho and wondered where he was. He hoped Idaho hadn't been hurt in the fight. If only he'd listened when Idaho wanted to wait. If he hadn't panicked. This would be his first night without Idaho since the day he'd run away. He closed the door, undressed, and got into bed.

He lay thinking of these people. The girl didn't like him. Mrs. McCumber was nice and she certainly could cook. He liked Frank McCumber. If he could stay a week he'd earn close to forty dollars. With that much it'd be "California, here I come." He hoped he'd find Idaho there somewhere. On that thought he went to sleep.

# 4

Tinkling bells woke Nick and pulled him to the window. In the early dawn a small, stocky man was driving a dozen cows up the road past the house. George was mincing out to the road. He fell in at the head of the procession and led them out of sight. Nick crawled back into bed and went to sleep.

He was awakened the second time by Frank McCumber's voice coming from the direction of the barn. This time he got up and dressed, making slow work of it because of his sore hands. When he stepped outside McCumber was coming from the barn with two pails of milk. They went to the house together.

After breakfast Norah McCumber insisted that he cover his hands again with lotion. "You keep the bottle," she said, "I'll get another in town this morning."

The family scurried about getting ready for church. Norah McCumber asked, "Would you like to go, Nick?"

Nick shook his head, "I haven't any clothes. I'll stay."

Frank McCumber said, "You can hold down the fort. We'll be back around noon."

"You're not going to leave him here alone?" Connie demanded.

McCumber said, very annoyed, "Connie! That's enough. Knock it off."

Nick watched them leave in the old sedan. Norah McCumber called, "Put more lotion on those hands. I'll bring a pair of gloves from town."

Nick smeared more lotion on his palms, got into his jacket, and set out to tour the McCumber acres. He visited the chicken house and the two hundred or so white birds. He wandered through the barn and the hay mow and looked into the grain bins. Then he went off across the pasture to walk among the giant trees. He scared up a pair of deer and watched them bound away. Pheasants took off like arrows. Quail exploded out of the grass at his feet. A raccoon climbed a tree and turned its black masked face to watch him pass. Dozens of small birds ducked about through the trees. Overhead a crow followed his progress for some time issueing a steady stream of complaints. The ground was spongy, the grass wet. Moisture hung from the ends of the fir needles and put a shine on the barren alder and maple limbs. In the darker spots the mustiness of decaying vegetation hung on the damp air. When he finally returned the McCumbers were driving into the yard. Mrs. McCumber had brought another bottle of lotion and a pair of heavy work gloves.

Next morning as they prepared to leave for work a stocky, black-haired boy came down the road and turned in at the lane. Frank McCumber introduced Nick to Tim Jessup. "The school bus stops here," he explained, "because the road's so rough. Tim and Connie are the last two riders so Tim hikes down to catch it."

Tim said, "Hello." His black eyes went over Nick then dismissed him. "You ready?" he asked Connie, "bus's due."

A minute later the bus, loaded with kids, turned in at the driveway and began backing around. Tim and Connie ran.

On the way to the logging site Nick rode the drawbar behind the seat. "Where's Tim live?" he shouted above the banging of the motor.

"Half mile or so above us. Their land joins ours."

"He's got funny eyes."

"How do you mean?"

"Black and sort of flat. Like you couldn't look into 'em."

"They're odd people. Henry Jessup and his sons, Tim and Lew, live alone in a big old house. Mrs. Jessup died long ago. Boys are a lot like the old man."

"Are they farmers?"

"Gyppo loggers."

"What's that?"

"Little independent operators who log tracts too small for the big outfits to bother with. They're always looking for work, usually on the verge of going broke."

"The Jessups like that?"

"Sure are. A couple of years ago Jessup thought he had a big logging contract all tied up. He went head over heels in debt to buy a lot of big machinery. Then he lost the contract. Now all he does with that expensive machinery is a little hard-scrabble logging on his own place. His timber's very poor. The good stuff was cut years ago. You'll likely meet him. He's been hounding me for months to let him log this place."

"Why?"

"To put that big machinery to work earning money. The gossip is that he's got some whopping payments to make."

It was the middle of the morning when Henry Jessup and his son Lew came by. Frank McCumber and Nick were taking a rest break sitting side by side on a log when the Jessups came through the trees.

Henry Jessup was tall, lean. He wore baggy bib overalls stuffed into the tops of knee-high rubber boots. His mackinaw coat was several sizes too big and hung sack-like from bony shoulders. An ancient, shapeless felt hat was pulled low over a shock of white hair. His flat, black eyes missed nothing. His gray stubble cheeks were puffed out like a squirrel's with his huge chew of tobacco. Lew was a carbon of his father only years younger.

Mr. McCumber introduced Nick and added, "Nick's visiting for a time."

Lew thumbed his hat back and looked at Nick. He pulled a knife from his pocket, pressed a button, and a gleaming six-inch blade shot out. He leaned against a stump and began idly jabbing the needle-like point into the bark. The act gave Nick a cold feeling in the pit of his stomach.

Jessup's eyes hit Nick momentarily, then dismissed him. He rolled the chew in his cheek, spit, and wiped his mouth with his hand. His voice was hearty and friendly, "Well, neighbor, you decided to sell us this timber and let us log it?"

McCumber shook his head, "I'm not interested. I told you before. I'm going to log it myself."

"So you did. With that piddlin' little old 'cat'?"

"I'll get a bigger one when I need it."

"You need it now." Jessup shook his head. "You don't make sense, neighbor. You'll be forever gettin' th' job done."

"I don't mind."

"What's that mean?"

"I'm in no hurry."

"Hm-m." Jessup spit again. "Tell you what, if you don't wanna sell th' timber to us, me and Lew'll move our big equipment in and do it on a contract basis. No sweat, no bother. You'll save th' expense of buyin' a big 'cat.' " He spread his arms expansively and smiled. "In a few months we'd have th' job done and you'd have your money, lots of it, right in hand. Spang! like that." He clapped his hands together. "No dribblin' along for years. You can't beat that."

"You can't if you're in a rush. But I'm not. I'm going to log my own way."

Jessup shook his head. "Your way's mighty slow. Mighty slow. Why, at th' rate you're goin' you'll never see th' end of it."

"You may be right."

"Course I am. Said yourself your missus wants a new house or an addition to th' old one. You need a new barn and outbuildin's. Now me and Lew and our big equipment can give 'em to you in a hurry, so's you and your family can enjoy 'em. So why stall?"

"I'm not stalling," McCumber said patiently. "Like I told you. I'm in no rush. I'll get the things I need as I go along."

Nick could see Jessup's hearty friendliness slipping.

He said bluntly, "You could be long dead before you get 'em. S'pose a log rolls on you like it done your boy? What about your wife and girl then?"

"It's a chance I'll have to take."

"Big chance. People get killed on little 'cats' like yours."

"I'll be careful," McCumber said.

Jessup chewed and spit. He got hold of that friendly air again, "Well, you think it over, neighbor. You think what it'd mean to you and your family if we came in and did this job and did it right. You think about it real good. I'll see you again." He started away calling over his shoulder, "Lew, let's get back to our own loggin'."

Lew closed the knife and ambled after his father.

"Acted like he didn't hear you say no," Nick said.

"That's old Henry Jessup for you. Every old-timer in the valley steers clear of him. I've never figured out if he can't hear, or doesn't want to, or if he doesn't believe what he's heard," Frank McCumber said.

"He acted friendly."

"That's his 'good neighbor' act. He always puts it on when he wants something. He'll be back. We'll go through this same rigmarole again."

"The same thing?"

"He may change the approach, but he'll be after the same thing, to log this stand of timber. Maybe he figures that eventually he'll wear me down or catch me in a weak moment and I'll say yes. He's made it work with others." He climbed on the tractor. "Let's go to work."

The day went smoother than the previous afternoon. The gloves saved Nick's hands. By the end of the day he had every move down pat. He knew exactly what Frank McCumber would do with the "cat." He could guess almost to the foot where to stand to miss a rolling log, then get in fast to catch it and walk it into the backwater. He kept having trouble hooking the cable so it wouldn't fly off. But by quitting time he had mastered that, too.

Their days fell into an easy pattern. Nick was usually wakened when Ad Nelson drove his cows up the road past the house. From habit he glanced out the window. Invariably George minced out to meet the cows. He dropped in at the head of the little procession and led them out of sight.

At a quarter to eight each morning Tim Jessup arrived to catch the bus with Connie. He seldom spoke to Nick.

Nick's relations with Connie did not improve. She had made up her mind about him the first morning. He liked Norah McCumber. She scolded him when he came in wet, mended his clothing, sewed on buttons, and nagged him to eat more. Working with Frank McCumber was as much pleasure as it had been with Idaho. When they took a rest break sitting side by side on a log the man had a way of talking that included Nick. It gave him a warm, grown-up feeling. Frank McCumber seemed to enjoy Nick's company, too. Coming in on the "cat" one night he began bellowing a logging ditty at the top of his lungs:

> "Oh, I eat when I'm hungry,
> I drink when I'm dry.
> If a log don't fall on me,
> I'll live till I die."

Norah McCumber called from the kitchen door, "Who's being tortured?"

"Tortured?" Frank McCumber exploded. "Woman, don't you know music when you hear it?"

"That's what it is?" She smiled. "Well, don't tell anyone and no one'll guess. I haven't heard you carry on like that for almost a year. You must feel good."

"I feel better than that," he shouted back.

Nick helped do chores. He let in the cows, fed them, put George in his stanchion, and gave him pellets. He even tried milking. Frank McCumber put him on Blackie, because she was an easy milker. The first night she kicked the bucket over. But Nick stayed with it. He was slow but by the fourth night he finished Blackie alone.

This was the last of winter. The days were often misty and foggy. Sometimes it rained all day and night without a break. It was wet and sloppy to work. But Nick didn't mind. Frank McCumber taught him to handle the "cat" and let him run it to and from the job. He even towed logs to the lip of the river bank. Once he tried rolling one into the water, but he almost lost the "cat" when his foot slipped on the clutch. He left that tricky part to the man.

Nick had earned almost forty dollars. He could go south in style. He thought often of Idaho and wondered where he was. In California, he hoped, lying under an orange tree enjoying that southern sunshine.

The first week passed. Frank McCumber said, "We're such a good team it's a shame to break it up so soon. Let's make it one more."

"Fine," Nick said.

Jessup and Lew returned. Nick listened to the old man go over the same arguments as if he hadn't presented them the week before. He put on his "good neighbor" act again. Nick felt Jessup was more intense this time. He waved his arms, chewed nervously at the cheekful of tobacco, and spit in all directions. Lew seemed not to listen to his father. He sat on a stump, the big knife in his hand, idly popping the blade in and out. Finally he snapped the blade shut and slid off the stump. "Pa," he said, "you might's well quit. You're wastin' your breath. McCumber's a bullhead. Can't you see that?"

Jessup shot a stream of tobacco juice and wiped his mouth. "He ain't seen the reason of it yet, son."

"He ain't goin' to. There's none so blind as those that won't see," Lew said. "Let's get back to our own loggin'."

"Lew's right," Frank McCumber said. "There's no

work here for you. You're wasting your time and mine. I'm going to select log this my own way in my own time. I don't need any more help and I don't want your big equipment in here. I hope once and for all I've made myself clear."

Jessup's sharp eyes studied Frank McCumber. He rubbed a hand across his mouth and rolled the chew into the other cheek. "Well, now. Well, now, I'll tell you somethin', neighbor. People change, conditions change. Maybe not today. But tomorrow's another day. If you change your mind, and I think you will, our equipment's sittin' right up there in th' yard. You remember that."

He walked off and Lew followed.

"His creditors must be hounding him pretty hard for money," Frank McCumber said thoughtfully. "He's not usually so insistent."

"If he needs work so bad why doesn't he log some of this other big timber around here?" Nick asked.

"It's all federal land. Nobody dares touch it. Mine's the only old timber claim not logged."

"Seems like Jessup had a good idea, if you want all the things he says you do," Nick said.

"I don't want him to log even one tree for me. Once he got his foot in the door I could have trouble getting him out. But there's another side, too. His big equipment would knock down every bush and tree on the place. I'd have two hundred acres of stumps, brush, and limbs four feet deep. It'd look like a battlefield. Then I'd have to hire him to clear it for another twenty-five or thirty thousand. The old fox is counting on that."

"You could farm it then."

"I'm farming it now."

"Logging's farming?"

"A forest's a crop, the same as wheat or corn. You just handle it differently. You harvest the whole grain crop each year, then plant another. A timber crop takes hundreds of years to grow. So the smart logger selective logs."

"What's that?"

"Cuts only the biggest and best trees, those that will make the most lumber and veneer. Let the small ones grow."

"These we're cutting aren't the biggest."

Frank McCumber smiled. "I'm taking these because that's all this little 'cat' will handle. When I save enough to buy a big 'cat' I'll start selective logging. That's where the money is." He pointed at a nearby tree. "That one's close to five feet in diameter. It's worth between five hundred and seven hundred dollars."

"For one tree?"

"That's right."

Nick thought of the number of such trees on this two hundred acres, "Why, this is a gold mine."

"Exactly. By selecting I can have a fine income as long as I live and still have a forest." He folded his arms and looked about. "A forest is alive, Nick. It's a living, breathing, growing thing. This forest was old before the first settlers crossed the plains. It's been home and refuge for countless generations of birds and wild animals. There aren't many stands like this left. It should not be slaughtered thoughtlessly in a mad rush to see how much money can be made in the shortest time. Harvesting these trees should be approached with the respect and dignity hundreds of years of growth deserve." He broke off a sliver and stuck it between his teeth. "If some in this valley heard that they'd think I was crazy."

Two days later they got the last logs into the backwater. Frank McCumber said, "It's not as big as I'd like. But let's call the tug anyway. We need the money."

Next morning the tug towed the raft to the sawmill.

Nick and Frank McCumber followed in the car.

Nick had never been inside a sawmill. While Frank McCumber was in the office he wandered about and watched logs being turned into lumber.

When they returned to the car Frank McCumber scowled. "The raft brought sixteen hundred dollars. I was hoping it'd be at least two thousand. I can see I won't be able to harvest enough small timber to buy the kind of 'cat' I need for big stuff. I've got to figure some other way to raise money."

They drove into Jewel where Frank McCumber went into the bank. When he returned he handed Nick ninety dollars and said, "Payday."

"This's more than I earned."

"A little bonus for a good worker."

It hit Nick with a shock that this was the end of his job. "I guess you're through with me," he said and felt a sense of loss at leaving.

"I'd like to keep you," Frank McCumber said, "but I can't afford it and I can't ask you to stay for nothing. I'm set for the next couple of weeks with those limbs and tree tops to clean up. I can do that alone. Besides," he said, smiling, "I know you're anxious to get to those orange groves."

"Yes," Nick said. He'd come to like the two hundred acres of timber, the barn, cows, chicken house, Mr. and Mrs. McCumber, and even that dumb George. But he couldn't offer to stay, even for nothing, without being asked. "I'll leave right away."

"This time ride the cushions."

"I'd like that."

"How'll you go, train or bus?"

"Bus. It's cheaper."

"One leaves tonight at six. I'll bring you in."

They were silent on the ride back. For the first time they'd run out of conversation.

Dinner was unusually quiet. Norah McCumber finally said, "I wish you weren't going. You be sure to write."

"I will."

"Don't just say it. I know boys. Do it. We want to know what you're doing and how you're making out."

"I'll write," he promised.

Connie glanced at him several times but said nothing.

"If you get into any difficulties let us know," Frank McCumber said. "Maybe we can help."

"Thanks," Nick said.

"Your shirts and extra jeans are washed and pressed," Norah McCumber told him. "There's an old suitcase of Frank's you can take."

All too soon dinner was over. It was time for Nick to pack his few belongings. He was rising when the knock came at the front door.

Norah McCumber answered it. The first thing Nick saw was the shine of a police badge on a tan jacket.

"Why, Cal!" Norah McCumber said, "what a nice surprise."

"Hello, Norah." The sheriff's voice was deep. He smiled at Connie. "How's my favorite girl friend?"

"Fine," Connie said. "How's my favorite boy friend?"

"Couldn't be better."

Frank McCumber said, "Cal, this's Nick Lyons. He's visiting us. Sheriff Cal Perkins, Nick."

Nick's hand was almost lost in the sheriff's huge paw. His voice was friendly, "How you making out with these hillbilly friends of mine, Nick?"

"Fine," Nick said.

"What brings you here?" Frank McCumber asked.

"Came to see you."

"I'm honored. What can I do for you?"

Perkins turned his hat uncomfortably in big hands. "You took some logs to the mill today?"

"Sure. I told you in the bank this morning."

"Any idea how many were in that bunch?"

"Forty-five, fifty. I didn't count 'em."

"You've been taking in quite a few lately."

"I want a new 'cat,' a new barn. Norah and Connie want a new house. Why?"

"Seems all those logs today weren't yours."

Frank McCumber sat up straight. "What's that?"

"They found four logs in the middle of your raft wearing Jessup's brand. Any idea how they got there?"

"That can't be," Norah McCumber said indignantly.

"I saw them." Perkins looked at Frank McCumber. "I know you didn't steal 'em. But how'd they get there?"

Frank McCumber shook his head. "You're sure, Cal?"

"Dead sure."

"How'd they find them? Normally pond men or sawyers pay no attention to brands."

"Jessup notified all mills to be on the lookout for his brand. Seems he's been losing logs. Could they have drifted in amongst yours?"

"I don't see how."

"Could you somehow have branded your own with a J?"

"I've only got one branding hammer. It's MC. I can't explain it, Cal. But if those logs wore Jessup's brand they were his. I'll pay for them."

"I wish that'd settle it," Perkins said.

"Why can't it?" Norah McCumber asked. "If Frank pays for the logs. That ends it."

"Not quite. Somebody seems to think the law's been broken, that there's log stealing going on. You know how these people look on log stealing, like ranchers do on rustling. Frank, I don't like to do this, but you'd better get your hat and come with me."

Nick saw Frank McCumber's hands tighten on the chair arms, his body go tense.

"Easy, Frank," Perkins said quietly. "Don't do something we'll both regret. I'm on your side all the way."

Norah McCumber's face was white, "You're going to take Frank to jail! He'll . . . be behind bars!"

Connie jumped up crying, "No! No! You can't! You can't!"

"Wait a minute," Perkins soothed. "Calm down. Now we know this's a mistake. But it's got to be cleared up. I'm not going to put Frank in jail. He's my friend. He'll sleep on the extra cot in the jail office."

Frank McCumber rose, "You're right. Norah, Connie, simmer down. This's a crazy mistake. It'll be straightened out in jig time." He looked at Nick. "Would you mind waiting a day or so and taking care of things until I get back?"

"Of course not," Nick said.

"I'll get my hat and coat."

They stood in the doorway and watched the two men go out to the police car. Frank McCumber called cheerfully, "Everything'll be fine. I'll be home sometime tomorrow." Then he got into the car and they drove away.

Norah McCumber closed the door and leaned against it. The room seemed very quiet. The fire crackled merrily. She folded her arms and looked about bewildered and frightened. "I'm scared," she said in a small voice.

Connie began to cry.

# 5

Milking two cows was the hardest job Nick had ever done. It took almost an hour and his hands and forearms were numb. After breakfast he turned the cows out, cleaned the barn and spent the rest of the morning servicing the "cat" and getting it ready to go again. By noon Frank McCumber had not returned. Norah McCumber said, "If he's not here by three o'clock I'm going in to see what's happening."

An hour later while Nick was splitting fireplace wood Sheriff Perkins drove into the yard. Frank McCumber was not with him.

Nick went into the house. The sheriff said "Hello" to Nick and went on talking to Norah McCumber. "I thought this was just a stupid mistake that could be cleared up in a couple of hours. But it isn't. It's beginning to look serious. You'd better get a lawyer for Frank."

"But Frank didn't steal those logs."

"I can't find a thing that says he couldn't have. You'd better get that lawyer."

"You believe he did?"

"I didn't say that. You've got to begin thinking how you're going to defend him."

Norah McCumber bit her lips, her blue eyes thoughtful. "All Jessup wants is the money for his logs, isn't it?"

"Norah, I've been around Henry Jessup for twenty years. The only things I know about him for sure are that he loves money and always wants his own way."

"If he'll take the money he can't prosecute. And if he doesn't prosecute—there's no case, is there?"

"That's right."

"Will you go up to Jessup's with me?"

"Of course." Perkins turned to Nick. "You'd better come, too. We might need a witness."

Old Man Jessup was tinkering around a tractor in a yard full of machines. There were several "cats" that made Frank McCumber's look like a toy. Nick noticed trucks, heavy trailers, a long-boomed log loader, and another machine he couldn't identify. Off a hundred yards or so was the river. An old scarred tug was tied to a piling. Lew was not in sight.

Jessup clumped over in boots, all smiles. He shifted the chew of tobacco in his cheek, spit, and said heartily, "Well, well, Mrs. McCumber! This's a real pleasant surprise. Yes, sir, real pleasant. What can I do for you?"

Norah McCumber came right to the point. "Frank's in jail accused of stealing four of your logs. Of course you know he didn't."

Jessup smiled his most friendly smile. "Mrs. McCumber, I don't know a thing except what th' police and mill told me. I hope you're right. But those logs were found in his raft."

"I know that. Maybe someday we'll learn how it happened. Right now all you want is the money for those logs and we can forget the whole thing." Norah McCumber took out a checkbook.

Jessup rolled the chew in his cheek and said thoughtfully, "Normally that'd be so. But not this time."

"Why not?" Norah McCumber asked.

"This here's a loggin' area. Has been for fifty years, maybe more. Why, when I came here those hills was one big forest top to bottom. Some of th' biggest trees that ever grew were taken outa here. Now look at those hills, all logged off. Th' valley floor's got th' only timber left."

"Mr. Jessup, will you get to the point?" Norah McCumber asked, annoyed.

"Comin' to it. Timber brought people to this area. They think loggin' and logs. Stealin' logs is a mighty serious offense around here. If I take th' money and drop charges people are gonna think I'm winkin' at log stealin'. That I was bought off. I can't have that."

"Practically no one knows about this yet," Norah McCumber said. "I'll pay you double the value of those logs. You can set their value."

Jessup rolled the tobacco in his cheek again. "That's right generous, but it wouldn't hardly be right."

"You want more money?"

"It ain't that. Th' law's been broke."

"It's been broken by someone, but not by Frank. How much do you want to drop this case, Mr. Jessup?"

Jessup shook his head and scowled at Perkins. "You bring her up here to try to buy me off, Cal? I don't like that. You're an officer of th' law, sworn to uphold it. Bringin' her up here in an official car and all don't look good. It don't look good at all."

"You're right," Perkins said calmly, "I am sworn to uphold the law. My job is also to help people any way I can. Mrs. McCumber wanted to talk to you, to make this suggestion. There's no harm in it. It's been done many times and we both know it. No one's trying to pressure you into anything. Say no and we'll leave. But to me this is a sensible way out of an awkward situation. If it goes to a trial it'll be expensive and some innocent people can be hurt."

"Way I see it," Jessup said, "th' law's been broke. It's up to th' law to set it right, not you or me. What'd people think if I start backin' up now? No sireeee. Law's got to take its course. That's what we got laws for."

"You're saying you want Frank to go to jail for four measly logs," Norah McCumber said angrily.

"It's th' principle of th' thing. Not them four logs. I'm sorry for you and Frank. I really am. But it's outa my hands. Completely out."

"Do you know what this publicity can do to us?"

"Frank shoulda thought of that, shouldn't he?"

Norah McCumber glared at him, then turned on her heel and walked away.

No one spoke on the drive back. They were turning into the yard when Perkins said, "No figuring that old geezer. There's only one thing sure about him. He'll do what you least expect. From past experience I'd have bet he'd take the money. He's that hungry for it. Then he comes up with this morality sermon." He shook his head.

"Is he really such an upstanding citizen?" Norah McCumber asked.

"He never was before."

"What do I do now?"

"Get that lawyer. I can recommend one. Charles Vickers. He's expensive, but good."

Mr. Vickers was small, middle-aged, and energetic. He wore gold-rimmed glasses and had a precise way of speaking. He spent all morning talking with Norah McCumber. In the afternoon he had Nick take him over the logging site and explain every move they made cutting a tree, trimming it, hauling it to the river, and putting it into the raft.

Nick had to attend the trial as a witness. Norah McCumber cleaned and pressed his pants and coat and lent him one of her son's shirts and a tie.

Connie begged to go, so her mother let her stay out of school. The three sat together in the courtroom.

Old Man Jessup was there, freshly shaved and dressed in a wrinkled blue suit. He kept rubbing a hand across his mouth as if he missed his chew of tobacco. Lew sat beside him. He had his knife in hand and was absently snapping the long blade in and out. Jessup finally whispered to him and he put the knife away.

Frank McCumber was escorted in by Sheriff Perkins. His eyes swept the room, found them, and he smiled. He sat down with Mr. Vickers.

Nick listened closely as Mr. Vickers led Frank McCumber through his testimony. It was almost what he'd told Cal Perkins at the house.

Nick didn't like the way the prosecuting lawyer badgered Frank McCumber. "You admit those logs could not have drifted into your backwater and into your raft. Someone had to put them there."

"Yes," Frank McCumber said.

"And you didn't do it. Then who else besides yourself could benefit by putting them there? Who, Mr. McCumber?"

Frank McCumber looked angry and bewildered but he finally said, "No one, I guess."

"Wouldn't the middle of a raft be the most logical place to put them if someone wanted them to go unnoticed?"

"I suppose so."

"How long did it take you to make up that raft? A month? Two months?"

"About a month."

"Do you ever go out on the raft while you're making it up?"

"Every time you put a log in. Three, four, maybe five times a day."

"You passed over and around those logs each time and didn't notice anything strange—like a different brand?"

"I wasn't expecting anything strange. I took it for granted they were all mine."

"I'm told you're a very good logger. I find it hard to believe a man of your experience wouldn't at some time notice four good-sized logs wearing a strange brand."

"I didn't," Frank McCumber insisted.

The prosecutor quizzed Frank McCumber on why he was cutting the small timber. He wrung from him the admission that he was short of money and that the extra Jessup logs would certainly help financially. By the time he finished Frank McCumber was red-faced and angry.

Nick felt Norah McCumber added nothing to her husband's defense. The prosecutor quizzed her hard about financial matters, how they managed to get along, how they planned to get the money for the new machinery he needed.

Nick was nervous when his turn came. He was afraid someone might ask where he was from or what he was doing at the McCumbers. But they seemed to take his being there for granted. Mr. Vickers led him carefully through his work with Frank McCumber and everything Nick had shown him the day he visited the logging site.

But when the prosecutor took over he felt he did no better than Norah McCumber.

"Did Frank McCumber discuss with you how he planned to get money to buy a bigger 'cat'?"

"Yes, sir. From the small timber he cut."

"Did he seem worried?"

"Well, he wanted a new 'cat.' "

"Did he ever say how he planned to raise money if he didn't sell enough small timber?"

"No."
"What did he say?"
Nick glanced at Frank McCumber.
"What did he say?" the prosecutor pressed.
Nick swallowed. "That he'd have to figure some other way. But he didn't mean stealing a few of Jessup's logs."
"What makes you so sure?"
"I was with him all the time."
"I see. Tell me, if you were going to steal logs would you do it in broad daylight or at night?"
"Night, I guess."
"Why?"
There was only one answer. "You could be seen in daylight."
"Logging's pretty hard work for a young boy. I imagine you're tired at night."
"Yes, sir."
"What time do you turn in?"
"About nine o'clock."
"Sleep well?"
"Yes, sir."
"Then between nine o'clock and when you get up in the morning you've no idea what goes on."
He'd been trapped. His heart sank.
Old Man Jessup put on a subdued "good neighbor" act when he was on the stand. He didn't want to harm the McCumbers. They were good neighbors. But the law had been broken. A log or two he'd not have complained. But four was more than he could afford to lose.
"This has happened before?"

"About a month ago the mill found one of my logs in McCumber's raft."

"Why didn't you complain then?"

"Didn't wanta blow th' whistle on a neighbor."

Mr. Vickers tried to shake Jessup's story, but couldn't.

Mr. Paulson, from the mill, verified that the log had been found, that Jessup refused to do anything about it. They had checked other incoming rafts for Jessup's brand, because he'd reported losing logs. None had been found in any but McCumber's rafts.

Nick felt the thin web of evidence drawing tighter around Frank McCumber. It reminded him of a fly caught helpless in a spider web. Old Man Jessup was the spider. It seemed everything was on Jessup's side and nothing on Frank McCumber's.

The guilty verdict didn't surprise Nick. The sentence did. Frank McCumber had to pay for the four logs, the court costs, and spend two months in jail.

Norah McCumber was stunned. Her face was white, her lips pressed together until they were bloodless. Connie's eyes filled with tears but she didn't cry.

Henry Jessup came up to them looking concerned. "I'm sorry, Ma'am. I didn't figure they'd go so hard on Frank. I'm really sorry."

"I'll bet you are!" Norah McCumber said in a tight voice.

Jessup shook his head. "He shouldn't of took them logs."

"Frank never took a chip that didn't belong to him. And you know it."

"Court says he did," Jessup said kindly. "But I understand you feelin' like you do. I admire you standin' up for Frank no matter what." He passed on up the aisle.

Cal Perkins arranged for Connie and her mother to see Frank alone in a small room off the courtroom. Nick waited outside. When they came out Connie was crying. Norah McCumber looked grim.

Perkins motioned to Nick. "Frank wants to see you."

Frank McCumber looked tired, bewildered. He shook hands and they sat down. "I wanted to talk to you alone." He passed a hand across his face. "Seems like a bad dream. I can't believe it happened."

"Maybe it didn't."

"What?"

"Maybe those logs never were in the raft. Somebody lied for a reason you don't know."

"They were there. Cal saw them and he's honest. All I know for sure is that I had nothing to do with Jessup's logs."

"I know that," Nick said. "I wish I could have said something that helped."

"It seems nobody can help me," Frank McCumber muttered. "But that part's over. It's the next two months that's bothering me. That's why I wanted to see you. I know you're anxious to get south into those orange groves. I wonder if you'd mind postponing your leave until I get out? The place needs a man around to split wood and milk the cows. Just look after the whole shebang. I can't pay you until I get out. The money we got for the raft is all the extra cash we've got. Most of it will go for lawyer's fees, court costs, and paying for the logs. If you don't feel you can stay I'll understand, and forget I asked."

"I haven't had much experience," Nick said. "I've never worked alone. You really think I can do it?"

"I'd bet my bottom dollar on it."

The blue eyes of the boy and the gray eyes of the man looked steadily into each other. Nick felt such a sense of pride at this responsibility as he'd never known before. "I'm in no rush," he said. "I'll stay as long as you need me."

Frank McCumber squeezed his hand until he winced. "I knew you would. Remember the first night I told you I believed things happened for a reason? I wondered what brought you to our place. Now I know. You've taken a big load off my mind. I can do this two months standing on my head."

Cal Perkins walked down the hall with Nick. "I'm glad you're staying," he said. "If you run into problems, holler."

"Thanks," Nick said.

"I want you to know," Perkins added, "Frank's not going to prison or anything like that. He won't be behind bars. He's going straight to a place called an honor farm where he'll work the next two months."

"I'm glad," Nick said.

They drove home in silence. Connie cried quietly beside her mother in the front seat. By the time they turned up the lane she'd had her cry out.

Norah McCumber put the car away, then she faced them and said in a business-like voice, "Now we're going to go on just as if Dad were away on business. Do you understand, Connie?"

"I can't," Connie said and began to cry again. "I

can't go to school and face the other kids. I can't."

"You can and you will," Norah McCumber said. "If your father were guilty that would be something else. But he isn't. If it gets too rough at school you let me know and I'll take over. Understand?"

"I'll try." Connie sniffed.

Norah McCumber turned to Nick, "I'm glad you're staying. I know Frank is, too." She turned toward the house, her back ramrod stiff.

Connie glared at Nick. "Why don't you get out?" she said in a low, angry voice. "We don't need you. We don't want you."

"You don't," Nick said. "Your mother and father do."

"I can do everything until Dad gets back."

"I can see you milking cows and cutting wood."

"I can learn."

"And lose a hand or foot. You've had three years to learn and didn't."

"How can you keep hanging around when people don't want you?"

"Not people," Nick said. "You! I'm hanging around, as you call it, because your dad asked me to. He's worried about you and your mother staying out here alone."

"A lot you can do. A tramp, a bum."

"Your father thinks I can. I guess I think more of him than you do."

"What does that mean?" Connie bristled.

"My staying keeps him from worrying, so I'll be here until he comes home. You want me to leave. So I guess you don't care much how he feels." With that he walked off to the barn.

Nick put feed in the mangers for the cows and let them in. He heard the jingle of bells and went to the door. George was leading Ad Nelson's cows home. Ad waved and Nick waved back. George turned up the lane and minced importantly to the barn and went to his little stall.

Nick leaned against the barn door and thought of Frank McCumber and all there was to do here. He wondered if he could manage alone. He wished Idaho were here.

# 6

Nick watched Connie and Tim Jessup next morning when the dark-haired boy arrived to wait for the bus. Connie was tense. She kept giving Tim worried looks. Tim didn't ask any questions about Frank McCumber and Nick had the feeling he talked of other things more than usual.

After the bus was gone Nick cleaned out the barn. He'd just finished when Jessup's battered pickup drove into the yard. Nick was close enough to see the surprise on Norah McCumber's face when she opened the door. But he could not hear what was said. After a minute she stepped aside and Jessup entered the kitchen.

Nick wondered what the old man was after and how he had the nerve to come here. As long as he was taking Frank McCumber's place around here he felt he should know what Jessup was up to. He went to the house.

The moment Nick stepped through the kitchen door he saw Jessup was putting on his "good neighbor" act. He smiled at Nick and asked in his heartiest voice, "Well, boy. How goes the farming this morning?"

"All right," Nick said.

"Got the cows milked and the barn cleaned?"

"Yes."

"I guess you ain't had too much experience doin' that."

"I've had enough."

Jessup's smile did not get into his black eyes and Nick knew the old man was annoyed that he'd intruded. "I was talkin' to th' lady, son. If you don't mind."

"Nick can hear anything you say." Norah McCumber's cheeks were flushed, her gray eyes angry. "Nick has taken over while Frank's away."

"Kinda young, ain't he?" Jessup asked.

"We don't think so. Now then, Mr. Jessup, you were saying."

"Yeah, well." Jessup ran his tongue around his cheek feeling for the chew that wasn't there. "As I was sayin', it's gonna be tough sledding while Frank's away," he said in his most friendly, sympathetic voice. "Frank didn't have money to throw around. And trial expenses and things take money. Probably all th' ready cash you had. Frank told me he wants to do selective loggin'. And as loggin's your only real income, so to speak, I was thinkin' that maybe me and Lew could help."

"How could you help?" Norah McCumber asked.

"Why, we could move our big equipment in here and log say twenty or thirty acres for you in jig time. Know how much you'd have if we did, Ma'am?"

"I've no idea."

"Maybe ten, fifteen thousand dollars cash in hand to tide you over till Frank gets home," Jessup said grandly.

Norah McCumber said nothing but Nick could guess how that sum tempted her. He said quickly, "We don't need it, Mr. Jessup. I'm going to do some logging. We'll have enough to get along."

Jessup's black eyes were angry. "I was talkin' to th' lady, boy. Maybe you've taken over runnin' th' farm part. I'm talkin' about loggin'. She makes th' decisions when her man's not around."

"Any decisions I make include Nick," Norah McCumber said.

"He's talkin' wild," Jessup said. "He don't know a thing about loggin' or he'd know no man can do it alone. And for sure a kid can't."

"It'll be slow," Nick said. "But I can do it."

"You're crazy, boy. You never handled a 'cat,' felled a tree, or anything."

"I can do it," Nick insisted.

Jessup snorted. "You lettin' a kid make important decisions for you?" he asked Norah McCumber.

She smiled. "If Nick says he can do it, I'm convinced he can."

Jessup's "good neighbor" act disappeared. "He'll get killed," he snapped. "Mark my word. Your man couldn't do it alone and he was a man and knew loggin'. How do you expect a green kid to do it?"

"He will," Norah McCumber said confidently. She seemed to be enjoying Jessup's anger and frustration. "I've great confidence in Nick. So has Frank."

"He'll get killed same as your boy was. You want his blood on your hands?"

Norah McCumber's chin came up. She said in the coldest possible voice, "Maybe you'd better take a good look at your own hands and see how dirty they are. If Nick wants to try, that's our business. I didn't ask you down here." She opened the door. "Good-bye."

Jessup tried to get hold of his temper. "You're makin' a mistake, Ma'am. A big mistake. I came here in good faith, a neighbor tryin' to help out while your man's gone. That's all. You think over my offer. Ten, fifteen thousand cash money in hand. You think hard on that."

"I've given it all the thought I'm going to. Good day."

Jessup shook his head and stalked out. "Try to be a good neighbor and people don't appreciate it," he grumbled.

"I've had all your good neighbor policy I can stand," Norah McCumber snapped and slammed the door.

The pickup rattled away. Then Norah McCumber said angrily, "The nerve of that old man! The colossal nerve of him! But I was tempted, Nick. Ten or fifteen thousand dollars. Whew!" She ran her hands nervously over her hair. "I was checking things this morning. That old man is absolutely uncanny. He's figured things exactly the way I have and I've got the facts. He must spend a lot of time keeping tabs on us. By the time I pay lawyer's fees and Jessup for the logs that sixteen hundred dollars will be mostly gone." She bit her lips, eyes troubled. "Maybe I should have let him come in and log a few acres."

"Mr. McCumber doesn't want him in here to cut even one tree," Nick said. "It'd be like letting him get a foot in the door. Once in, there could be trouble getting him out. That's why I said what I did."

"I know, and I appreciate it. He did catch me in an awfully weak moment this morning. Why, I'll bet that old fox planned it that way. I feel as you and Frank do about Jessup. But we're going to need money, Nick. Not a lot, but some."

Nick spoke without really thinking and to comfort her. Afterward he was as surprised at his words as Norah McCumber was. "I'm going to log some of that little stuff."

Norah McCumber looked at him. "You weren't bluffing," she said. "You really meant it."

And then he knew he had. "I can do it," he said. "I know I can."

"No! no!" She shook her head. "You could get hurt. We'll find another way to raise money to tide us over until Frank comes home."

"What other way?"

She ran hands through her hair. "I'll think of something. I've got to."

"I do it or you let Jessup come in here. There's no other way. We both know it."

She shook her head, "It's too dangerous for a boy. Jessup's right there."

"I tell you I can do it," Nick insisted. "It'll be slow."

"Frank wouldn't let you if he were here. Neither will I."

"Yes, he would," Nick said quietly.

"What makes you think so?"

"He told me. What do you think we talked about all the time I was in the room with him after the trial?"

"Why, taking care of the place, milking, things like that. You weren't in there long."

"Too long to talk about milking and splitting wood. You were upset. You weren't keeping track of time."

"I was certainly upset. What did you talk about?"

"Milking, things like that. Then he told me how the raft money would be almost all gone. He was worried. I suggested a little logging to keep the family going and he agreed."

She gave him a straight look. "I don't think I believe that, Nick."

"It's true," Nick lied. "He didn't agree right off. He said the same thing you and Jessup did. But after we talked about it a little he said I should go ahead and try. But if I ran into trouble I was to quit."

"Frank said it like that? That you could try? You're sure, Nick?"

"Just like that," Nick said.

"Well, Frank should know. But I'm surprised he'd let you try alone."

"I've worked with him more than two weeks," Nick pointed out. "He showed me everything as we went along."

"If you got hurt I'd never forgive myself. Neither would Frank. And it can happen so fast."

"Accidents always happen fast. Have you ever seen a street accident?"

"Logging isn't like crossing a street." Norah McCumber smiled. "It's much more dangerous."

"Did you ever cross against the light in Chicago?"

"Well, no."

"I have, lots of times."

"All right," she agreed. "You can try on one condition. You take no chances. None at all. If a thing looks the least bit dangerous you don't do it. Agreed?"

"Agreed," Nick said.

"Mr. Jessup's going to be most unhappy," she said, her gray eyes beginning to twinkle.

Nick got the "cat" out and went up the dirt road to the logging site. Frank McCumber had said he was going to pile brush and clear up the mess before he did more logging. So Nick began on that.

He had problems handling the blade. He lowered it too far, gouged ditches in the earth, and covered limbs and brush. He got the "cat" stuck and it took an hour to free it. Then he didn't get the blade low enough and ran over limbs, breaking them up. It was past noon before he felt he had the blade under any kind of control. By night he was going fine and had cleaned up over an acre. One more day, he figured, would clean it up.

Late the next afternoon Old Man Jessup and Lew came. Nick was working on the last of the brush when he saw them. How long they'd been there he didn't know. Lew was sitting on a stump, hat pushed back on his black hair. He had the knife out and was idly jabbing the point into the bark while his emotionless eyes watched Nick. Jessup leaned against another stump, long arms folded, scowling, working at the eternal chew of tobacco. Nick stopped the "cat" and idled the motor.

Jessup rolled the tobacco in his cheek, spit, and said, "You really figure to do some loggin'." He was not in his "good neighbor" mood.

"That's right," Nick said.

"Probably kill yourself first."

Lew jabbed the knife point hard into the bark, twisted, and broke out a huge sliver. "Yeah, you'll likely kill yourself."

"Takin' a big chance," Jessup said. "Boy with no more experience than you."

"I'll make out," Nick said.

"Not th' way you're handlin' that 'cat,' " Lew said.

"Mrs. McCumber payin' you to do this?" Jessup asked.

"I'm not worrying about pay," Nick evaded.

"She ain't." Jessup rolled the chew in his cheek and considered Nick. "I've lived in this valley more'n fifty years. Know most everybody. I never heard of you."

Nick said nothing.

"Where'd you say you was from?"

"Small place off a-ways," Nick said vaguely.

"Only some kind of relative would do this for nothin'," Jessup probed.

"I guess so."

"You a relative?"

"Sort of," Nick said.

"You are or you ain't," Jessup said, annoyed.

Lew slipped off the stump, put the knife away, and said, "Come on, Pa. Let th' dumb kid kill himself."

Jessup's eyes dug into Nick and the boy could see the old man was angry that his probing had been thwarted. "I ain't quite figured you out yet, boy," he said. "But I will. I will." They went off through the trees.

Nick's palms were wet on the steering levers. His heart was hammering. Lew and that knife gave him the chills. But Old Man Jessup, he felt, was even more dangerous.

Nick finished the cleanup that night. Next morning he began selecting and marking the trees he planned to fell. He tried to do it as he thought Frank McCumber would, taking the biggest he could handle and leaving the others to grow. He even marked with chalk on the tree the direction he wanted each tree to fall, so it would not damage young trees.

Nick felled the first two trees exactly where he'd planned. The third twisted, came back at him, and pinched the blade. He jumped aside. The tree crashed almost where he'd been standing. The saw was wedged tight, the chain broken. He returned to the house for the second saw and cut the wedged one free. Hereafter he'd have to study the lean of the tree to determine its fall. He felled three that day, trimmed off the limbs, and cut off the tops. He got three more the following day. Then he began dragging them to the river.

Getting the logs into the water was the tricky part.

He'd almost lost the "cat" in the river that other time when his foot slipped on the clutch. He'd have to be especially careful. Nick figured he could start the log down the bank with the "cat," jump off, run down with the pike pole, and catch it in the river before the current got a grip on it.

He eased the "cat" against the log and began to push. The log reached the lip of the bank. Another foot. He crept the "cat" forward. Suddenly the log bounded away. He set the brake, jumped off, grabbed the pike pole, and raced after it. It was already bobbing beyond reach, thirty or forty dollars gone.

Nick shut off the "cat," sat on the bank, and thought the problem through. He solved it with a length of rope. He tied one end around the log, the other to a tree, leaving just enough slack for the log to hit the water. He didn't lose another log. Thereafter he'd fell six trees, trim off limbs and tops, then haul them to the river and put them into the backwater.

Several times Norah McCumber came out to watch. She was pleased and surprised. "Frank couldn't do any better," she said, "you're going great guns."

But each morning as he left the house she cautioned him to be careful. "Mind, Nick," she said, "no risks."

Connie said little to Nick. He felt she still looked at him with suspicion and disapproval. She fed the chickens and gathered the eggs. Sometimes she came into the barn to pet George for a few minutes. Only once did she admit to trouble at school. When her mother asked, her chin set and her eyes flashed. "A little at first. But it's over. I handled it." Norah McCumber smiled and asked no more.

The number of logs in the backwater slowly grew. Jessup came once, leaned against a stump, chewed tobacco, and watched. Nick was trimming limbs off a downed tree and pretended not to see him. The saw sputtered on an empty tank and he shut it off. Jessup said, "I see you're still at it."

"Yes, sir," Nick said.

"Goin' mighty slow. You've only got fifteen, twenty logs in th' pond so far."

"That's right." Nick screwed the gas cap off and began filling the tank.

"How much McCumber payin' you?"

"I'll know when I'm through."

"Contract work, eh?"

"Is that what they call it?"

The black eyes studied Nick. The old man's questioning took a different turn. "Who'd you say you were?"

"Nick Lyons."

"I know that. You don't give out much information, boy."

"There's not much to give," Nick said.

Jessup rolled the chew in his cheek. "You're a funny kid. Yes, sir, a real funny kid. Ain't quite figured you out yet."

The gas tank was full. Nick screwed the cap on, gave the rope a pull, and the motor began to snarl. He went to work again. When he glanced up a minute later Jessup was gone.

At the end of two weeks Nick thought he had enough to call out the tug from the mill. He was there when it came and he felt a thrill of pride as the tug eased his raft out and headed for the mill.

That afternoon Nick and Norah McCumber went to the mill office. Norah said, "I think you should go in and get the check. But have them make it out to me so I can cash it."

When Nick returned he handed her a check for six hundred and ten dollars. "I thought it'd be more," he said.

She smiled and ruffled his hair, her eyes shining. "Sounds just like Frank. You know, I sided with Mr. Jessup in this business of you logging alone. I was very skeptical and plenty worried. If Frank hadn't believed in you I'd never have consented. Wait till I tell him when I see him Sunday."

"Maybe you'd better not," Nick said.

"Why not? He'll be proud as punch."

"He might not," Nick said. "I lied to you. We never talked about me logging, just doing chores and looking after things."

"You deliberately lied to me?"

"I sure did."

"Well! That's the nicest fib I've ever been told. Let's you and me go put this check in the bank."

Norah McCumber was quiet on the drive home. She ran the car into the garage, shut off the motor, and sat scowling.

"Anything wrong?" Nick asked.

"There's plenty wrong. And it's been wrong since the day you came. You've taken over this family and done everything, just as Allen would have. And you're still sleeping in the shed."

"Nothing wrong with that."

"Everything's wrong with it and we're going to correct it now. Come on, you're moving into Allen's room."

"I'd rather not. Mr. McCumber told me how you and Connie feel."

"Nick," her gray eyes were dark, "Allen's been dead a year. It's high time I accepted that fact."

"Connie won't like it."

"It's time she accepted it, too. And she's got to get over this phobia that everybody who's ridden a freight train is a no-good murdering tramp. Maybe this will help. Come on, let's get busy."

It was the first room Nick had ever had to himself. After Norah McCumber left he stood in the center of it and looked about. The furniture was old, but well kept. A Jewel High pennant was on one wall with a football picture. He wondered which was Allen. A twenty-two rifle leaned in a corner.

The school bus stopped out front. He heard Connie's shouted, "See you tomorrow." Then the back door slammed.

Nick went to the window and looked out. The sky was dark. It was going to rain. He looked down on the shed, the barn and corral, the two hundred acres of virgin timber beyond. He felt good about his logging and the money it had brought. He remembered Idaho telling about the good feeling Cap Small got helping someone. He knew what Idaho meant now. This room was final proof that he was taking care of the place just about as it should be done.

# 7

Nick didn't learn what Norah McCumber said to Connie, but when he came downstairs she avoided looking at him. Nick paid no attention to her and went out to do chores.

After supper they were sitting in the living room. Norah McCumber was mending, Connie was studying, and Nick was reading an outdoor magazine when a knock came at the front door. Norah opened it to Cal Perkins.

Perkins said, "Hello, Norah. How're things going? Been meaning to stop by. Just don't seem to find time."

"Things are fine," Norah McCumber said. "Nick's been logging, alone. Today we sold six hundred dollars' worth of logs."

"You did it alone?" Perkins looked at Nick.

"He certainly did. Isn't that something?"

"It sure is." Perkins smiled. "Frank'll be glad to hear that. Incidentally he's doing fine. Saw him the other day. He's pushing a crew planting about a million fir seedlings on burned-over land." Then the smile left his face. "I always seem to be the bearer of bad tidings." He handed Norah McCumber a folded paper, "This's a subpoena, ordering you and Nick to appear before Judge Sam Murdock's juvenile court Monday morning."

Fear that was near panic hit Nick like a fist smashed into his stomach.

Norah McCumber said, "A subpoena? I don't understand."

Cal Perkins explained. "A petition has been filed by a very, shall we say 'civic-minded citizen,' declaring that Nick is a juvenile without family or relatives and should therefore be declared a ward of the court."

Norah McCumber's gray eyes began to sparkle angrily. "Would this 'civic-minded citizen' be named Jessup?"

"How did you guess?"

"But why? What business is it of his?"

Perkins shook his head. "He's a born snoop. Always has been. Why, he's been known to go down to the courthouse and get copies of people's wills and show them around. Couldn't possibly gain him a thing. He seems to want to make everybody's business his business. That's the main reason all that expensive logging machinery is sitting idle around his house. He's too well known. People don't trust him."

"That old reprobate," Norah McCumber said angrily. "He needs to have his nose twisted."

"That he does. But don't sell him short," Perkins

warned. "He's got more devious sides than you can shake a stick at."

"How did he learn about Nick? We didn't tell anyone."

"He asks questions, he surmises, he pieces bits together until a picture begins to emerge. Then he guesses at the rest. Nick's a stranger here. He's living with you folks. There's been no explanation about him being a relative or old friend. That's enough to start a man like Jessup wondering. He's like a hunting dog sniffing out a trail."

"He's a two-faced snoop."

"That's right," Perkins agreed. "But both of you be there at ten A.M. for the hearing. Incidentally, I'm appearing as a character witness for the McCumbers and Nick."

"What will they do to me?" Nick asked fearfully.

"I can't say. Not jail or anything like that. You've committed no crime."

"Will I have to go to some orphan or foster home?"

"Possibly, but I can't really say. You'll find Judge Murdock a very fair man."

"Nick might have to leave here?" Connie asked.

"It's possible."

"Don't we have anything to say about it?" Norah McCumber demanded.

"Of course, both you and Nick. That's what the hearing's for, to give the judge the full picture."

"Old Jessup will be there, of course."

"Naturally, he signed the petition."

"I don't like it," Norah McCumber said flatly.

"Most people don't. But you be there."

"We'll be there. Can't we stop that old man from trying to persecute us?"

"Everything he's done so far as I know is legal, Norah."

"That's just the trouble," Norah McCumber said.

After Perkins left, Connie resumed studying. But she kept stealing glances at Nick.

Nick's mind was in wild turmoil. He thought he'd run far enough to get away from this. He had to be alone to think. He rose and said, "Guess I'll turn in."

Norah McCumber said, "It's going to be all right, Nick. We'll have our say. And Cal will be there."

"Sure," Nick said and climbed the stairs.

He lay on the bed. Shock and the feeling of being trapped kept rolling over him. He tried to calm his thinking, to reason. But he kept remembering Willy Lanier. Willy'd been in two foster homes when he ran away and returned to the neighborhood. Nick talked with him before they caught him the third time. "Neither of those homes kept me because they wanted me," Willy said bitterly. "All they were interested in was the money they got for keeping me. Anything's better'n that."

Having Cal Perkins appear as a character witness wasn't going to help. Neither would having their say. Frank McCumber had his say in court, too. In spite of his innocence he was in jail.

Nick rose and stared out the window at the night. It had begun to rain. He could see the black shine of the lane road. George was nibbling on a bush near the house. He had to get away from here. Now—tonight! He had to run again. An odd thought came to him. He wouldn't spend even one night in the first real room of his own he'd ever had.

Nick sat on the bed, took off his right shoe, and spread the ninety dollars Frank McCumber had paid him carefully along the sole. He was committed now to leaving. Maybe he'd find Idaho in California. Good old Idaho. He sat quietly on the bed and waited for Norah McCumber and Connie to go to bed.

Connie came first. He could tell by the light run of her feet. Norah McCumber followed. Her footsteps hesitated at Nick's door. Then they went down the hall.

Nick gave them a half hour to get to bed and, he hoped, to sleep. Then, wearing his coat and cap and carrying his shoes, he tiptoed down the stairs and left the house.

George had disappeared.

Nick turned up his collar and struck out down the road toward Jewel.

A railroad trestle crossed a canyon on the outskirts of town. The train would creep across it. Nick went under the trestle, found a square of old sheet metal, leaned it against a trestle leg, and sat under it out of the rain. The near panic that had claimed him for several hours was wearing off. He could think again.

By morning he should be several hundred miles away, out of the clutches of Judge Murdock's juvenile court. He hoped this next freight was heading south. If not he'd go north and double back. He could drop off at a town and catch a bus all the way to California. Thanks to Frank McCumber he could ride the cushions.

Frank McCumber had been a lot like Idaho—a friend when he needed one.

A disturbing thought began to bother Nick. He tried to push it away but it would not be denied. He'd promised Frank McCumber he'd look after things until he was released. McCumber was counting on him and he was running out just as he had on Idaho that night in the boxcar.

But he wouldn't go to an institution. He'd run too far, too long to be caught now.

He wasn't really deserting them. He'd taken care of things. Cutting six hundred dollars' worth of logs had done the job. Norah McCumber had more than enough money to see them through. They didn't need him. They could get Ad Nelson to milk. There was fireplace wood cut and Connie could talk Tim Jessup into splitting a few blocks. If he went before Judge Murdock there was little doubt he'd be sent away. So they'd wind up without him anyway.

Two men slid down the bank. Nick moved over and said, "There's plenty of room under here."

They crowded in with him and sat down. One asked, "Where you headin'?"

"California," Nick said.

"Now there's the country," the other said with a sigh. "Good old California. Orange groves, sunshine. This next freight's goin' south."

"Why anybody stays up here in the cold and rain is beyond me," the first said.

The rails began to hum. They climbed the bank and waited beside the track. Far down the headlight beam cut the night. "California," one of the men laughed, "here we come."

The engine crept past out onto the dark trestle. The train was a long one. Cars moved slowly by. They watched for an open door.

"There! Let's go!" They ran and climbed aboard. One of them yelled at Nick, "Hey, shake a leg before she hits the trestle."

Nick didn't answer. He watched the cars crawl past until the last one vanished in the night. Then he went down the bank and took the road back to the McCumbers.

The weeks had done something to the boy who'd run in panic in Chicago. That boy couldn't have handled a "cat" or a chain saw. He'd not have cut six hundred dollars' worth of logs and sent them to the mill. Running was for frightened boys.

The meeting in Judge Murdock's office was very informal. Judge Murdock was a graying man about fifty. He had a friendly smile that immediately put Nick at ease.

Henry Jessup was there in his old rumpled suit. He kept rubbing a hand across his mouth and Nick knew he wanted a chew of tobacco.

Cal raised a finger in greeting as Nick and Norah McCumber entered.

When they were seated the judge said, "Now, Nick, do you know what this is about?"

"Yes, sir," Nick said.

"Good. It's going to be very informal. I want to hear from everyone."

He talked with Norah McCumber first. She told him how Nick had come to their place and gone to work for them. "Frank likes him," she said. "We all do. Nick's a lot like—like our son was. We'd like him to stay." She explained how Nick took care of the place while Frank McCumber was away, that he'd logged six hundred dollars' worth of timber all by himself. "He's just a boy, your honor, but he's taken over like a man."

"Where is Mr. McCumber now?"

Norah McCumber hesitated, then finally told the whole story. "Frank didn't take those logs," she ended. "It was some kind of crazy accident."

"I see," Judge Murdock said.

Nick tried to read something in the judge's face, or his voice, or the kind of questions he asked. But Judge Murdock showed him nothing. His voice was calm, unhurried, impersonal. "You say everyone in the family likes Nick. Does that include your daughter?"

"Well, no," Norah McCumber admitted. "But you have to understand about Connie. Ever since that murder near our home she's had this phobia about anyone she thinks might be a tramp. She was never like this before. She'll get over it but it's going to take a little time."

"At the moment she doesn't like Nick."

"That's right," Norah McCumber admitted.

Cal Perkins could do no more than corroborate Norah McCumber's testimony. He added that he'd known Frank McCumber since they'd moved here and found him an upright, decent citizen. He praised Nick's logging and the way he'd taken over in Frank McCumber's absence.

Henry Jessup was next. He rubbed a hand across

his mouth and began in his most reasonable "good neighbor" voice. Nick was amazed at the things the old man knew about him. He knew of his mother's death, that Nick had run away from the Chicago juvenile authorities, and of his travels about the country with Idaho. "No tellin' what kind of scrapes th' boy's got into hangin' out with a man like that, your honor. A tramp, a bum most of his whole life." Jessup knew about the fight in the boxcar. "All tramps—and probably drunk, your honor. You know how these tramps are."

"No, tell me," Judge Murdock said quietly.

"Well," Jessup rubbed a hand across his mouth, taken by surprise. "Well, your honor, they just ram around th' country doin' mostly nothin'," he said vaguely. "They've got no homes, no families. They don't want any. They spend their lives livin' off other people one way or another, beggin', stealin'."

"Don't we all live off each other one way or another?"

"I hadn't thought of it like that," Jessup confessed.

"Go on, Mr. Jessup."

"Well, sir, this kid says he jumped outa the boxcar and ran away because he was scared. Maybe yes. Maybe no. Maybe he had somethin' else up his sleeve."

"Like what?"

"Well, he hikes up that old loggin' road where McCumbers and us live. I'm wonderin' why."

"Why do you think, Mr. Jessup?"

"Who knows, your honor? Who can say what kinda mischief a kid who hung out with tramps, learnin' their ways, doing Lord-only-knows-what these past months, has got in mind? He came from the tough side of a tough city. There's no way checkin' where he's been or what he's done. One thing I know for sure. He's a bum, a tramp. He's been in tough company so he's a tough kid. Not the kind a family should take in. And certainly not one with just two women and no man around."

"You were doing your civic duty turning him in?"

"Absolutely. I don't want another murder like we had last year."

"So far Nick seems to have done very well at the McCumbers. Suppose he's taken away. There are things a couple of women can't do. Then what?"

"Why, me and the boys'll be right down to help. We figured to all along. We're neighbors, neighbors look out for each other. They wouldn't want for a thing. As for ready cash I've already offered to take my big equipment in there and log fifteen or twenty acres for Mrs. McCumber. That'd give her ten, maybe fifteen thousand dollars to see her through till her man comes home."

"Then there's nothing personal in your signing this petition?"

"No, sir. I just don't want anything to happen to Mrs. McCumber and her daughter. They've had trouble enough. Anything I can do to make it easier for them I will."

"I see," Judge Murdock said.

The old man's act went over, Nick thought angrily. The judge couldn't help but be impressed.

Judge Murdock consulted a paper, then he looked

at Nick. "I've a little sketchy material about you. Apparently you've never been in trouble, lived with your mother. You were in the third year high school when she died. Why don't you fill me in on the rest? Why did you pull up and leave? Where have you been, with whom? What did you do up to the time you arrived at the McCumbers? And relax, Nick. This isn't a trial in any sense. Take all the time you want and tell it any way you like."

Nick's nervousness passed as he began to talk. He told Judge Murdock everything, from the moment the welfare woman got out of the car to the weeks he'd spent with Idaho, the things they'd done, places they'd worked. How much money he'd made. How Idaho got them jobs, the things Idaho taught him.

"You got into no trouble?"

"Only that night in the boxcar. That was my fault. I was supposed to stay awake. I didn't."

"Do you remember any names and addresses of these people you worked for?"

Nick gave him a few names of towns, first names of people. But no addresses. "I didn't pay any attention," he said. "Idaho always knew them."

"He knew a lot of people?"

"He knew somebody at every town and farm we stopped at."

"Does it bother you that Connie McCumber doesn't like you?"

"A little," Nick admitted. "But after what happened I don't blame her."

"What do you plan to do when Mr. McCumber returns?"

"Go to California."

"Any plans for more school, or will you bum around the country the rest of your life?"

"I hadn't planned anything. I was going with Idaho. He was taking care of everything."

"Did he ever suggest anything to you?"

Nick smiled, remembering. "He said a man should light someplace, put down roots, have a home and friends he could talk with over the back fence. He said there was more to living than watching the world go past an open boxcar door."

"I'd say he put it very well." Judge Murdock seemed to forget Nick then. He sat scowling at the paper on his desk.

Nick's heart sank. He should have caught that freight with the other men. He'd be in California now. Like it had been with Frank McCumber, there was too much on Old Man Jessup's side and nothing much on his.

Judge Murdock said thoughtfully, "I understand how you feel, Mrs. McCumber, and I sympathize with you. I can also understand how your daughter feels." He glanced at Henry Jessup. "I hope I can understand how Mr. Jessup would want this matter cleared up. Such a situation can present problems. Nick, shouldering the responsibilities of the place and logging alone is commendable. But he is a minor with no relatives to speak of." He frowned and looked at Nick. "I don't doubt anything you've told me. But I wish we could verify the things you've told me, the people you were with, places you were, and specifically things you did while traveling around the country with this Idaho."

Perkins said, "Your honor, there was supposed to be another witness, who I believe could corroborate the things Nick has told you."

"Where is this witness?"

"I don't know, your honor. Perhaps if we could take an hour's recess. . . ."

Judge Murdock shook his head. "I'm hearing another case this afternoon. We'll have to go on."

The door behind Nick opened. A quiet voice said, "Possibly I can shed some light on this, your honor. May I come in?"

"Of course," Judge Murdock said.

Nick twisted about. His heart gave a thunderous leap, then began to race. The man wore a red plaid jacket. He had heavy, muscular shoulders. His bullet-shaped head was completely bald. He was smiling. The smile got into his warm brown eyes.

Judge Murdock's calm voice asked, "And you are . . . ?"

"Peter Jamieson, your honor. But most folks just call me Idaho."

# 8

Nick forgot where he was. He jumped up crying, "Idaho! Idaho!" The next moment his hand was lost in Idaho's big hard palm and Idaho's warm brown eyes were smiling down at him. Words tumbled from Nick. "Where've you been, Idaho? How'd you get away from those men in the boxcar? I panicked, Idaho. I ran out on you."

"Easy," Idaho soothed. "Relax, partner. We'll talk later. We've got a lot of catching up to do. Right now I have business with his honor here. So take it easy until we get through."

Nick remembered where he was and sat down, embarrassed.

Idaho took the chair in front of Judge Murdock's desk, put his hat on the floor, crossed his legs, and waited for the judge's questions. He was the same old smiling, friendly Idaho. And yet he wasn't. This man was completely calm, relaxed before the impressive dignity of the surroundings and Judge Murdock. For all the concern he showed he might have been a lawyer sitting there, or even another judge. He had the air of one who knew exactly what was expected of him. A tremendous pride swelled in Nick.

"Now, then," Judge Murdock said, "I understand you can shed more light on Nick, Mr. er, Idaho." He smiled.

"I believe so, your honor. I can tell you all about him from the night he left Chicago until he landed here."

"That's the period I'd like covered," Judge Murdock said. "Go right ahead."

Nick listened, amazed at Idaho's memory for people's names, places, dates, length of time they worked, what they did, the amount of money they earned. Idaho covered practically every day of their time together. He recounted things they'd talked about: Nick's fear of being sent to a home, his desire to get to California's orange groves.

"He was with you wherever you went?" Judge Murdock asked. "You didn't leave him for a few days?"

Idaho shook his head. "Not once, your honor. Nick was as green as they come. I had to keep him with me, show him everything." Idaho smiled at Nick. "Seems he's learned quite a bit lately on his own."

When Idaho finished the judge said, "That seems to corroborate everything Nick's told us only in much more detail. Now suppose you tell us a little about yourself. Where do you live?"

Idaho looked surprised. "Why, I live all over."

"I mean where is your home?"

Idaho shook his head. "I've no home as such." He smiled. "I'm what you might call a free soul, your honor. I answer to no special job or clock. I go whenever and wherever fancy strikes me and the railroad usually takes me there. Mostly I migrate with the ducks and geese, north in summer, south in winter. When they start to fly so do I."

"Ever been in trouble with the law?"

"I've always tried to avoid that. But I was once, five years ago I was mistaken for another man in Springfield, Missouri. Two days later the mistake was discovered and I was released from jail."

"Nothing else?"

"A few traffic tickets when I drove trucks for farms or ranches. It was usually for a burned-out headlight or an overload. Nothing else."

All during this talk Old Man Jessup had been fidgeting, rubbing a hand across his face, running his tongue around his cheek as though searching for his chew. Now he could restrain himself no longer. "Your honor, you ain't takin' this man's word for anythin', are you? Why, he's nothin' but a bum, a tramp, a hobo. Has been all his life. He admits it. I bet if you check back you'll find plenty of jails he's been in. We've only got his word for what he's been doin'. Who knows what sneaky tricks he's taught this kid? One thing sure, no hobo makes a respectable and honest livin'. Seems to me he oughta be checked out good before any of this stuff's believed."

"You have a point, Mr. Jessup," the judge agreed. He looked at Idaho.

Idaho nodded. "I expected I'd have to show some stability of character and prove the statements I've made. I've simply never been a man who could stand living any length of time in one place, your honor. But just because I move about the country freely and at whim is no indication I haven't lived an otherwise normal and useful life." He drew a number of small books from his pocket and placed them on the judge's desk. "These may help answer some of Mr. Jessup's questions."

The judge looked at them. "Why, these are bank books," he said surprised. "There are five here."

"That's correct, your honor. And you'll notice those books are from banks in five different states. They're records of accounts I have in each bank."

Judge Murdock thumbed through the books murmuring, "Hm-m-m, hm-m-m." He looked at Idaho. "Very sizable accounts. I expect you can explain them?"

"I never carry a great deal of money with me so I set up accounts in those different states."

"For a man who rides the railroad, there's a lot of money represented here."

"My expenses are small," Idaho explained. "Mostly clothes and food. And often food and board are included where I work. Moving about the country I stop and work regularly and I've always been lucky enough to command top wages. In some thirty-five years a man can acquire a sizable chunk of money. Also several bankers have been good enough to suggest investments that have done well."

"How do we know that, your honor?" Jessup interrupted. "His say don't mean a thing. We got no proof he didn't rob banks and stores and things. Maybe he even stole those books and made the entries."

"Call any of those banks and ask about me," Idaho suggested. "I'll pay for the calls."

Judge Murdock selected two books and handed them to Perkins. "Call these, Sheriff."

Perkins disappeared into an inner office.

The judge said to Idaho, "Nick told us about the fight in the boxcar and how he jumped out. Did you do the same? And why did you stay in Jewel?"

"I got away from those fellows in the car and jumped the same as Nick did. But I lost my money in the fight. I know now Nick jumped a mile or so north of Jewel. I was about the same distance south. I was afraid he'd been hurt so I hiked back to look for him. Next morning I asked around town but nobody had seen a strange boy answering his description. I figured he'd gone on, hitch-hiking the highway. I was broke and needed a stake. Paulson's mill needed a man on the graveyard shift. I had no idea Nick was in the area until I came to work last night and heard the talk about log stealing and a sixteen-year-old boy who had cut a raft alone. I talked to Sheriff Perkins and he verified that it was Nick. He told me about the hearing today. And here I am."

Perkins returned and handed the bank books to Judge Murdock. "I called both banks, your honor. A Mr. Canby at one said, 'If Idaho wants to buy something, sell it to him. He's good for it.' The other was a Mr. Nicholson." Perkins smiled at Idaho. "He said to remind you that you owed him the biggest dinner in town. It seems that Mr. Jamieson invested some money at Mr. Nicholson's suggestion."

"That I did," Idaho said. "Nicholson's a vice president. He suggested I buy stock in a new shopping center. I told him if it paid off as well as he thought I'd buy him the biggest and best dinner in town. So it has. That's good."

"How do I know you talked to them banks?" Jessup demanded. "Or that both those fellers are what they said they are? How do you know for sure without seein' them?"

"Oh, come now, Mr. Jessup," Judge Murdock said, "that's getting pretty far afield." He handed the bank books to Idaho. "I'm satisfied that Mr. Jamieson, er, Idaho, is exactly what he says he is."

"I ain't," Jessup exploded. "Just because a couple of bankers say he's okay don't say where he got all that money. He could have robbed someplace and then put it in th' bank. No way tellin' where money comes from or how it was got."

"I'm not going to argue with you," Judge Murdock said coolly. "You'll have to abide by my decision, Mr. Jessup. I accept the things that have been said about Mr. Jamieson, Idaho. And therefore what he's said and these other folks have told us about Nick and his conduct."

Jessup opened his mouth to object but Judge Murdock went on. "Now then, we have here a boy under age, with no relatives, no home. He's been in no trouble. He's taken over a two hundred acre place in the absence of the owner and not only kept everything operating smoothly, has logged six hundred dollars' worth of timber alone. No small accomplishment. Yet he is a minor and the law is specific about that. So this is what I'm going to do. I'll take no action whatever at this time. Nick is to return to the ranch with Mrs. McCumber. He'll go right on taking care of things as in the past until Mr. McCumber comes home. At that time we'll meet here to decide what's best for Nick. In a sense, I'm releasing Nick to Mrs. McCumber, and also to Sheriff Perkins. I'll expect you to stop by and look in on Nick now and then, Sheriff."

Cal Perkins nodded. "I will, your honor."

"You can't do that!" Jessup burst out.

"Oh?" Judge Murdock looked coldly across the desk at Jessup.

"What I mean," Jessup stammered, "th' kid's a minor, like you said. It don't seem right leavin' him out there—a kid like him. After all he's just a tramp, so's this Idaho. If th' kid stays Idaho'll likely be out there, too. It's downright dangerous for that woman and young girl."

"Mr. Jessup," Murdock said, "you've got all the mileage you're going to with that 'bum and tramp' talk. I've looked into your standing in this valley, too." He smiled at Nick then. "Keep up the good work, son."

Sheriff Perkins opened the door and they all filed into the hall.

Jessup stomped off angrily.

Idaho punched Nick in the shoulder, his brown eyes smiling. "Well, partner. It's good to see you again. You've changed some."

"I weigh about the same," Nick said.

"I mean in here." Idaho tapped his chest. "You've been growin' up. It shows. Workin' for the

McCumbers has been good for you. Nothing like shouldering responsibility to make a boy grow up."

"I don't know what we'd have done without Nick," Norah McCumber said.

Idaho scowled after the retreating Henry Jessup. "Some people are nosy out of curiosity," he said, "others have a reason. I wonder what that old man's reason is."

"You think he has one?" Norah asked.

"Man doesn't usually flare up like he did in there just because his curiosity's been punctured."

"That old man might," Perkins said.

"I've heard talk about him," Idaho observed. "He's got quite a reputation as a local wheeler-dealer, a fast-buck artist."

"That's him to a T," Perkins said.

Nick had been watching Idaho closely. "You didn't get hurt fighting those men in the boxcar?"

"A few bumps and bruises and lost my money somehow."

"I lost mine, too. It was my fault. And I should have stayed and helped. When you needed me I lost my head and ran out on you. I'm sorry, Idaho."

"No need to be," Idaho said. "Gettin' outa that car was plain smart. I jumped, too, soon as I got the chance." He stifled a yawn. "Came down here right from work. Haven't had any sleep yet," he explained. "Guess I'd better get back to the boarding house and hit the sack." He smiled at Nick. "I didn't have to worry about you, partner. You've been doing just fine."

"Thanks to all you taught me."

"Not about loggin'."

"Mr. McCumber taught me that. You'd like him."

"I'll bet I would."

"When will I see you again?"

"Not today. I'll likely sleep most all afternoon. I'll be out tomorrow around one, two o'clock."

"I'll drive in and get you," Norah McCumber offered.

"Thanks, but there's no telling just when I'll wake up. I can hike out in half an hour or so. Hike'll do me good."

They watched him go off down the corridor and Norah McCumber said, "He's an amazing man. I don't blame you for liking him. I do, too."

Norah was quiet most of the way home. Finally she said, "Just wait till Connie gets home. I've got things to say to that young lady."

"What things?" Nick asked.

"Old Man Jessup had facts about you he couldn't have guessed. He got that information just one way. You told us. It came to him from Connie."

"I don't think Connie talks to him," Nick said.

"I don't mean Jessup pumped Connie, though he's not above it. But Connie told Tim, or Tim pumped Connie and told his father. Either way, that daughter of mine's the guilty person. Old Jessup played up that bum and tramp business and the murder of the Grahams exactly the way Connie's always harping on it."

"I wish you wouldn't say anything to her," Nick said. "She can't help the way she feels."

"She's got to get over that crazy phobia or it'll affect her whole life."

"Jumping on her won't help. Anyway, everything turned out all right."

"Yes, it did, didn't it? All right, I won't say anything for the present. But it better not happen again," she said darkly. After a minute she smiled at Nick. "I'm glad you came back the other night." When Nick looked surprised she went on. "You hit a couple of stair treads that creaked. I watched you go down the lane and much later I saw you come back. What made you change your mind?"

"I ran out on Idaho that time when he needed me and I've felt bad ever since. You and Mr. McCumber have been good to me and I didn't want that same feeling with you that I had with Idaho."

"I'm glad you came back. Judge Murdock's a very fair person. You've nothing to fear from him."

"I know," Nick said. He didn't fear Judge Murdock, but what was going to happen to him when Frank McCumber came home?

# 9

Connie looked surprised when she returned from school and found Nick there. But she just tightened her mouth and said nothing. Later when she and her mother were doing dishes in the kitchen Nick heard her ask, "What did the judge say about Nick?"

"Not much," Norah McCumber said.

"Was Mr. Jessup there?"

"He was there and complained and shouted and tried to bully. But it didn't work. Idaho refuted nearly every statement Jessup made."

"You mean that tramp Nick ran around with was there?"

"He certainly was and he's no tramp."

"Then Nick's going to stay?"

"Until Dad comes home. Then we'll meet with Judge Murdock again to decide Nick's future."

Connie asked no more questions but she kept stealing glances at Nick all evening.

Next morning he was greasing the "cat" and changing the oil when Norah McCumber came out to ask what he was going to do.

"Thought I'd do some logging," he said.

"It's not necessary. We've plenty of money to tide us over until Frank comes home. I worried every day you were out there alone."

"I got along fine."

"I know. But I thought you might relax a little now. Just do chores and things like that."

"Mr. McCumber will start logging as soon as he gets home," Nick said. "I might as well go on with it. Besides, I enjoy it."

"You be awfully careful."

"I will."

After lunch Nick was getting ready to head for the logging site when Idaho came up the lane. "This's quite a place." He shoved back his hat. "I didn't expect a farm, too. How about giving an old pal the grand tour?"

"Sure," Nick said. He took Idaho through the barn, the sheds, the chicken house. Then they went up the "cat" road into the timber. Idaho kept looking at the big trees, muttering, "What monsters! You don't see many virgin stands like this any more." Rabbits bounced ahead of them. A squirrel ran halfway down a trunk and scolded at them. Pheasants exploded out of the grass. A covey of quail ran down the road to disappear like magic. "Why, there's a fortune here," Idaho said. "A fortune."

Nick explained how Frank McCumber planned to log selectively and the equipment he needed.

Idaho nodded. "Sure, sure. We're going to have to do a lot more of this throughout the nation. Sad to say, we've about seen the last of the great forests. If everybody believed like this McCumber it might be different. He sounds like a forward-thinkin' man. Don't make sense he'd steal four or five scrubby logs."

"He didn't."

"Facts say he did."

"The facts are wrong."

"He's in jail, partner."

"He doesn't belong there."

Idaho nodded. "It happens sometimes."

They came to the logging site, sat on a couple of stumps, and Nick explained how they selected trees, felled them, cut them into logs, got the logs into the river, and made up a raft.

Idaho listened and looked. "You did a fine job. I'm right proud of you." His brown eyes studied Nick. "You've changed more than I thought yesterday. The scared kid I helped into a boxcar in Chicago could never have done this. You're a young man and it's happened in a hurry. You know," he added thoughtfully, "this would be a nice place to stay, to put down those roots I told you about. You thought of that?"

"How come you brought that up?"

"It's plain you like it here. You like these people. And they like you or they wouldn't have kept you on. It looks like a perfect setup. Maybe when the man gets home they'll want you to stay. You know, California isn't all lyin' in the shade of an orange tree drinkin' orange juice."

Nick shook his head. "You can't tell people you want to stay; besides, Judge Murdock probably won't go for it. He's set to put me in a home if I appear before him again."

"Meaning you don't figure to appear."

Nick nodded. "The day Frank McCumber comes home I head for those orange groves."

"Could be you're makin' a mistake."

"I don't think so."

Idaho changed the subject, "Yesterday this Jessup kept harpin' about some murder around here. What was it?"

Nick told him about the Grahams and how the murderer passed Connie in the road and how she later had to identify him. "She's even afraid to pass the Graham house now," he said.

"That was a rough experience for a girl. Most always when people are afraid it's because they don't understand, or their imagination runs away with 'em. Imagination can do some odd things to you. When I was a kid I was afraid to go into a certain patch of woods because somebody once said they'd seen a wolf in there."

"Did you ever get over it?"

Idaho nodded. "In a funny way. I was hikin' one day and came home by a back route. Before I realized it I was in the middle of that woods. I expected to see slavoring wolves behind every tree. All I saw was a couple of rabbits and a squirrel. After that it became one of my favorite places. Maybe Connie should go to the Graham place and see for herself that it's just an empty house."

"She'll never do that."

"Then she's got a problem." Idaho stood up abruptly. "Now that you're in charge what do you plan to do until Mr. McCumber comes home?"

"Guess I'll start logging again tomorrow."

"I'll come help a few hours a day."

"That'd be great," Nick said. It was good to think Idaho and he would be working together again. "Only trouble is I broke one of the chain saws. I've only got one now."

"What happened?"

"I pinched it felling a tree and the chain broke. I don't know if the bar's bent or not."

"Let's go back and see. Maybe I can fix it."

The bar was sprung. Idaho spent the afternoon straightening it and repairing the chain.

Connie came at four. Nick introduced Idaho to her. She looked at him, her mouth tight and disapproving. Then she stalked into the house without a word.

"She likes me." Idaho smiled.

Idaho had supper with them. Afterward he went to the barn with Nick to milk. "You take one," he said. "I'll take the other."

"You can milk?" Nick asked.

"Jack of a lotta trades but master of none," Idaho said and reached for a milk pail.

George minced into the barn ahead of Connie, went to his small stall, and stood waiting for his pellets.

"Well," Idaho said, "an Angora goat. Been a long time since I saw one of these fellows. What's his name?"

"George," Connie said.

"What do you feed George, Connie?"

"Pellets from that sack." Connie pointed to a sack leaning against a bale of hay.

Idaho went to the sack, found a can, and bent over to fill it.

George whirled. His head went down.

Nick yelled, "Idaho, look out!" It was too late. George had exploded in full charge. He belted Idaho from behind and drove him head first over the bale of hay. Then he stood there shaking his horns and going, "Ba-a-a ha-a-a-a."

Nick and Connie ran to the bale of hay and leaned over. Nick asked, "Idaho, you all right? He hit you an awful wallop."

Idaho sat up groggily and felt his arms and legs. "Everything seems all right but my dignity." He glared at George. "I hope someday another goat does the same to you and see how you like it."

"I'll feed him," Connie said.

"I started to." Idaho scrambled up. "I intend to finish it." He carefully faced George, filled the pound can, and dumped it into the goat's box. "Eat your head off," Idaho grumbled, "I hope you get indigestion."

Connie left trying not to smile.

After they'd finished the chores Norah McCumber and Nick drove Idaho back to town. They invited Connie to go along and got a flat no.

Idaho arrived after lunch the next day and they went right to work. Idaho did the felling, Nick the trimming. They hauled each log to the river as they got it ready. It was like old times to Nick except that now he worked as a partner, not a helper. They didn't stop to rest until late afternoon.

They sat side by side on the "cat" tread and Idaho said, "This place reminds me of one I was at years ago. There was a young lady . . . I almost stayed." He kicked mud off a shoe and squinted at the sky. "Came awful close."

"Why didn't you?" Nick asked.

Idaho smiled. "Geese and ducks started flyin' over, headin' south for the winter. I had to follow."

"Did you ever go back?"

Idaho nodded. "Once. I thought about it all winter. Next spring on the way north I stopped. I heard in town the lady had married and was real happy. I didn't go near the place." He watched a chipmunk scamper along a limb. "It wouldn't have worked. I'd been beating the rods too many years to settle down." He slid off the tread. "This isn't putting any logs in the river."

Idaho didn't come every day, but even so the logs began forming into a raft in a surprising hurry. Connie remained outwardly unfriendly but Nick caught her covertly watching Idaho and frowning uncertainly. Nick guessed that she was beginning to come around, at least with Idaho.

Nick made friends with George. He took to carrying goat pellets in his pocket and George followed him around while Nick doled them out a couple at a time. He enjoyed hand feeding the goat and the velvety touch of his lips against his palm.

Within a week, with Idaho's help, the raft in the backwater was bigger than the one Nick had sent to the mill. One evening as they let Idaho out at his boarding house Norah McCumber said, "How am I going to pay you for all this work, Idaho?"

"Who's talking pay?" Idaho said. "I come to visit my partner. If we do a little loggin' at the same time, so much the better. I was never one to stand around. Nick's the one hired to work."

Norah McCumber shook her head. "Idaho," she chided, "you'll never be a rich man."

"Wrong," Idaho smiled, "I've got a thousand friends. My health's good. I've got some money in the bank. I've no worries worth mentioning and I can enjoy the same sunset and sunrise as a king. I am rich."

There came a night when George did not turn in at the lane as Ad Nelson drove his cows past. Nick thought nothing of it until Connie came into the barn looking for him. "He probably went on to the Nelsons again," Nick said. "When we take Idaho to town I'll stop on the way home and get him."

George was not at the Nelsons. Ad said he hadn't been in the pasture when he went for the cows.

At home Connie was immediately worried. "That long wool got caught in blackberry vines and is holding him fast."

"That can happen?" Nick asked.

"Oh, yes," Norah McCumber said. "Angoras have been known to become so tangled up they starved to death."

"I'll go look for him."

"Wait for me," Connie said. "I'll get the flashlight."

"You don't need to go."

"You don't know where the pasture is. I do. And I know every blackberry bush in it. I'm going."

She ran into the house and returned with the flashlight. They headed up the road. It was getting dusk. Shadows of trees and mountains came down heavy in the valley. Black clouds were blotting out the sky.

Connie said, "We've got to hurry. It'll be dark soon. And it's going to rain."

They passed Jessup's and about a quarter mile farther a vacant house that sat back a hundred or so feet from the road. Nick asked, "What's that place?"

Connie glanced up. "Grahams." She walked faster.

Nick looked at the house. It was big, two-storied. A lot of bric-a-brac around the eaves and porch gave it an air of old elegance. The windows were dark staring eyes. One had been broken. The paint was beginning to peel. There'd once been a lawn and cared-for shrubbery. Now the grass was a foot high and frost yellow. The shrubbery was beginning to sprawl in all directions. Behind the house were sagging fences and several outbuildings. In the light of what had happened there it did look forbidding.

Another ten minutes brought them to the big fenced pasture where Nelson's cows grazed all day. It was dotted with patches of blackberry vines.

Nick said, "Let's split up. You go left, I'll go right. Whoever finds George yell. We'll meet at the big tree in the center of the pasture."

They searched almost an hour, circling blackberry patches and calling. Nick found strands of Angora wool caught on thorns but no sign of George. It began to sprinkle. When they met at the tree it was dark and raining steadily.

"He's got to be someplace around here." Connie was close to tears.

"He's not in the pasture," Nick said. "Anyplace he might have gone?"

"There's another way he could go home. But he wouldn't."

"How do you know?"

"He never has."

"What's this other way?"

"The road makes almost a half circle getting here," Connie explained. "An old trail cuts from the back of this pasture past the Graham house, through a corner of Jessup's and comes out in our land. But he wouldn't go that way."

"He'd head for home, wouldn't he?"

"Yes."

"Is there any other way home?"

"No."

"How close does that trail come to the Graham house?" Nick asked suspiciously.

"It goes through the back yard."

"Then come on."

Connie bit her lips nervously, then she fell in beside him without a word.

The trail was almost overgrown in places with brush and weeds. Connie gave Nick the flashlight and he played the beam ahead of them. They came out of the brush and trees suddenly and were in the Grahams' back yard. Nick stopped and looked up at the house.

Connie said nervously, "Go on. What're you waiting for?"

Nick was remembering Idaho's words. Maybe

Connie should go in there and see it's just another vacant house. He caught Connie's hand and said, "Let's look through the window."

"No." Connie pulled back.

"Come on," Nick urged, "I just want to peek through the window."

"Why? It's just a house."

"That's right. But you've been talking about it ever since I came. I'm curious. Come on."

Connie allowed herself to be pulled up the steps and across the porch where they peered through a dusty window next to the kitchen door. It was black dark inside. Nick switched on the flashlight. There was a stove. A table with chairs around it stood in a corner. Dishes sat on the drainboard. A kettle was on the stove.

Nick reached for the kitchen door and found it open a crack. He pushed it wide and looked inside, swinging the light about.

At his shoulder Connie whispered fearfully, "That dark on the floor—that's blood!"

Nick turned the light beam down. Then he lifted it toward the ceiling and caught a steady stream of silvery drops. "Water," he said. "There's a hole in the roof. It's just water." He pulled Connie into the kitchen. They could hear the hollow drum of rain. Nick flashed the light around. An open door led into a dining room. An archway beyond opened into a living room. Furniture sat about. There was a tablecloth on the table, pictures on the walls. It looked like people had been gone just long enough for a film of dust to settle over everything. "Just a vacant house," Nick said.

"I'm getting out of here," Connie quavered.

Nick held her hand tight. "You're not listening. I said this is just an empty house. There's nobody in it. Quit being such a baby. Look around." He flashed the light about. "See. Nobody."

That moment they heard the steady thump, thump! It seemed to come from somewhere up near the ceiling in the dark living room. Nick froze. His heart rushed into his throat. Connie gasped, then both her hands clutched him in a fierce grip.

The sound came again—a steady, measured thump, thump that echoed through the black emptiness like the steady strokes of a hammer. Now it seemed to come from a far corner of the living room. Nick pointed the flashlight, held his breath, and pressed the button. The powerful beam picked out a stairway he'd missed before—and standing on the bottom step looking straight into the eye of the flashlight was George. He was calmly chewing on a bit of paper. He bobbed his head, shook his horns at them, and minced the length of the living room going "Um-m-m-m." He walked up to Nick and stuck his soft nose in his palm looking for goat pellets. Nick fished in his pocket, found a couple, and gave them to him.

Connie twisted her hands in his long wool and murmured, relieved and half angry, "You, you, George! I ought to beat you."

Nick said, "See, nobody here but George and us. The kitchen door was partly open. He came in and the wind blew it almost shut. He's probably been wandering around in here most of the day."

They went outside and entered the trail again. George trotted between them, bobbing his head, and shaking his horns as if he were leading the way home.

The rain increased to a hard, pelting drive. They ran out of trail and began cutting through the timber. They were hurrying, paying no attention to anything except where they put their feet when they almost ran into Old Man Jessup and Lew. They were standing in a little cleared spot directly in front of them. Nick figured later that if he hadn't had the light directed at the ground to keep them from tripping over roots and limbs, and if the Jessups hadn't been looking in the opposite direction they'd have been seen.

As it was Nick flicked off the light, sank behind a screen of brush and pulled Connie down with him. They had George between them and Connie held the goat with both hands twisted in his wool. "What're they doing?" she whispered.

"Search me," Nick whispered back. "But I'd as soon they didn't see us."

George pulled, trying to get loose. His hind foot hit a stick and it broke with a snap.

Lew instantly turned, "You hear that?"

"Hear what?"

"A stick bustin' like maybe somebody stepped on it or somethin'."

"Quit bein' so nervous," his father said. "Who'd be out here?"

"How'd I know? I tell you I heard somethin' and it's close."

"Probably a deer."

"When I see it I'll believe it." Lew began moving toward them kicking through the brush clumps. "No deer'd stand around makin' a noise like that. It was somethin' else. I wanna know what."

"You're worse'n an old woman," his father grumbled. "All right, we'll roust out whatever you heard—if you heard anything." He began kicking angrily through the brush as Lew was doing, grumbling, "Spend all our time and get soaked cause you've got the jitters. No wild animal's gonna hang around with us makin' this racket."

They were coming toward the bush behind which Nick, Connie, and George hid. Lew was only a few feet off when Nick saw that he had the wicked-looking knife in his hand. Any second he'd head straight for their bush.

Behind Lew Old Man Jessup kicked through a patch of brush, then bent over studying the ground.

It happened suddenly. George tore loose from Connie's hands and exploded right through their bush. His head was down. His hoofs churned. He'd drawn dead aim on Old Man Jessup bent over with his back to him.

Lew yelled, "Pa, look out!"

Jessup straightened and turned. Deprived of his target George stopped uncertainly. He shook his horns and stamped his feet and went "Ba-a-a-a."

Lew ran at him brandishing the knife. "You dumb goat," he said savagely, "I'm gonna cut your heart out."

Connie started to rise and Nick pulled her down.

Old Man Jessup picked up a stick and joined the attack. The two men tried to pin George between them. George's ears came forward. He backed away.

Lew lunged and George danced lightly aside. The old man took a mighty swing and missed. In exasperation he hurled the club at George. George leaped aside. The club rapped Lew across the legs and brought a howl, "Pa, watch what you're doin'!"

This was a game to George. He galloped around the clearing. Lew and the old man panted after him. Lew made a wild slash with the knife. George was not there. The old man aimed a mighty kick, grunting with effort. His feet shot from under him and he sprawled flat on his face. Lew kept chasing George but the goat stayed tantalizingly just beyond reach. George circled the clearing once more, leaped nimbly over Old Man Jessup who was trying to sit up, and galloped off through the trees toward home.

Lew chased him a few feet, then came back. "Told you I heard somethin'. That dumb goat. Someday I'll cut his throat from ear to ear." He helped his father up. The old man's face was black with dirt. He'd lost his hat. He kept gagging and groaning. "Pa, you all right?" Lew asked. "Pa, what's wrong?"

Between gags and groans the old man gasped, "Swallowed my chew. Goat made me swallow my chew. Ugh, I'm sick!"

Lew found his hat. "Come on, we're goin' home. No sense hangin' around here in the rain. With that goat loose somebody'll come lookin' for him sure. Let's get outa here."

As soon as the Jessups had disappeared Nick and Connie rose and quietly hurried away.

They found George in the barn waiting for his feed of pellets. Nick gave him a can and they both petted him and told him he'd done a fine job getting them out of trouble. Then they went to the house.

In the kitchen Norah McCumber asked, "Did you find George?"

"We found him," Nick said. "He's in the barn now eating." He and Connie looked at each other. Nick could tell they were both thinking the same thing. They began to smile. Then they burst out laughing. They laughed until the tears ran.

Norah McCumber looked at them amazed. "Well," she said finally, "it must be funny. Tell me so I can laugh, too."

Connie wiped her eyes, "You wouldn't believe it, Mom," she gasped. Then she and Nick were off on fresh gales of laughter.

Norah McCumber folded her arms and said thoughtfully, "I'll bet I wouldn't. I'll just bet I wouldn't."

# 10

Idaho showed up at the logging site shortly after noon and Nick told him about last night. Idaho chuckled. "That George is a character for sure. I'd like to have seen those two chasing him around in the rain." He became serious then. "Does seem odd their being out here in the dark and rain for no apparent good reason. And what they said seemed sort of odd, too."

Idaho took off his hat and scratched his bald head thoughtfully. "How far is it up there?"

"Not more than three hundred yards."

"Let's hike up and look around."

When they reached the spot Idaho stood in the center of the opening and looked about. "Queer sort of little clearing," he said.

"How do you mean?"

"Usually there's small trees around the edges of any clearing. This one has all big trees. No small stuff at all. Just unusual, that's all. Where could the

Jessups have been coming from or going to that would bring them through here?"

"The river's the only place."

"They got a boat?"

"An old one tied to the bank up near their house. They've got a small raft there, too. They do a little logging in their scrub timber."

"Does a fence separate the two properties?"

"No."

"Mighty easy to get onto somebody else's property with no fence," Idaho said.

"I suppose so. But why was Lew so jittery? And what did Mr. Jessup mean by saying that somebody would come looking for George, sure?"

"It was an odd statement, all right," Idaho agreed. "But there's no tellin' what they mighta been talking about before to make that logical. Anyway, it's not unusual for an owner to wander over his property to look around. It's mighty easy to get off when there's no fence to stop you. At night in the rain is a funny time to do it though." Idaho shook his head, baffled. "We might as well go back. There's sure nothing here to see."

They hadn't taken a dozen steps when Idaho stopped and asked, "You and Mr. McCumber been doin' some diggin' up here?"

"No, why?"

"Somebody has." Idaho pointed. Scattered through the low brush and deep grass were dozens of small holes that looked like someone had lifted out a spadeful of earth and grass.

"But why?" Nick asked.

Idaho didn't answer. He moved about kicking through the grass. "Quite a lot of diggin's been goin' on here, but you can hardly see the holes because of the long grass. Look around for a low mound of dirt or brush or grass."

"What's in it?"

"Not sure. Just look."

Nick came onto a mound of grass and twigs within a minute. He'd have paid no attention if he hadn't been looking for it. He kicked into it and turned up soft earth. He called Idaho.

Idaho scraped away the twigs and grass and a thin coating of dirt. He uncovered the top of a stump more than four feet across. The tree had been cut off just a few inches above the ground. Idaho jabbed into the top of the stump with his pocket knife. It was hard and solid. He scraped a spot clean, inspected it, then sat back on his heels and murmured, "Well, well, what do you know?"

"What?" Nick asked.

"Those shovel holes made me suspicious. I saw this done once a long time ago. A couple of fellows were stealing timber from government land. They'd sneak in at night, cut a tree, strip off the limbs, haul out the log, get rid of the limbs, and cover up the stump like this so nobody'd be suspicious. They got away with it for months before they were caught."

"You mean somebody's done that here?"

"Unless you and Mr. McCumber cut this tree and covered up the stump?"

Nick shook his head, "The old 'cat' wouldn't handle such a big log. And why would we cover up the stump?"

"Exactly! But somebody did so no one would know a tree had been cut."

"Oh," Nick said. Then the full significance dawned on him and he said again, "Oh!"

"This tree was cut within the past couple of weeks," Idaho went on. "Rain hasn't even settled the loose dirt yet. This made a good-sized peeler log, worth maybe six or seven hundred dollars."

"How'd they take it out?" Nick asked. "Dragging would gouge a deep ditch. And there's no 'cat' tracks. Besides, I'd have heard a 'cat' motor, and you can hear a chain saw for a mile."

"Let's take this one at a time," Idaho said. "They didn't drag it and they didn't use a 'cat.' They probably used a machine called a Lumberjack. It has huge, soft tires that leave no marks on the ground. You wouldn't hear the motor because they probably had a muffler on it. And they didn't use a chain saw. They used an old fashioned cross-cut that two men pulled by hand. Very little noise."

"What about the limbs and top?"

"The Lumberjack took them away. They're likely burned."

"What's a Lumberjack look like?"

"A huge tractor on wheels. In front it has a pair of big tongs, like lobster claws. It can pick up and walk off with a six-foot log twenty feet long without leaving a trace."

"A machine like that is sitting in Jessup's front yard.

"And the Jessups were right here last night. Maybe we'd better look around and see what else we can find."

They found five more covered stumps. "Could even be more someplace else," Idaho said. "But I'd guess these six represent around four thousand dollars' worth of high-grade logs. Let's cover 'em up again and get outa here. We don't want anybody to know we've found these."

They carefully covered the stumps and returned to the "cat" and their logging site. They sat on a log and Idaho said, "Let's see if we can figure out this mess. If I remember right you told me those logs Mr. McCumber was supposed to have stolen were found in the middle of your raft."

"That's right."

"And Jessup's got a lot of logging machinery parked around his place that's not paid for?"

"That's what Mr. McCumber said. Jessup thought he was getting a big logging contract and went into debt for all that machinery. Then he lost the contract. Mr. McCumber figured Jessup was hounding him to let him log this land so he'd earn the money to make payments. The company was about to foreclose on the equipment."

"And McCumber refused. Jessup, with his back against the wall, had to figure another way to get money in a hurry." Idaho broke off a sliver and stuck it in his mouth. "Heard lots of stories about that old man. Got more tricks than a fox." He tossed the sliver away, "Let's see if we can figure how he thinks."

Idaho shoved back his hat. "Logging this two hundred acres of timber is the answer to all his problems but the owner said no. So he has to figure another way to get in here. First off he's got to get rid of Frank McCumber. He floats a log down and puts it into a McCumber raft more than a month ago. Then he alerts the mills that he's losing logs and to be on the lookout for his brand. Paulson's mill finds the log."

"Why one log?"

"For two reasons. He laid the groundwork for bigger fish to fry. By refusing to prosecute on one log he's made himself the good guy. No one will question his motives when he springs the trap. He sneaks four logs into the next raft. He now has a legitimate reason for going to court. Nobody can overlook five stolen logs. Frank McCumber goes to jail. He's out of the way."

"I still don't see . . ." Nick began.

"There's no reason for the women to come up here. And you're just a kid. The coast is clear except for one thing. You do what he doesn't expect. You begin logging on your own. He's afraid you might stumble onto something so he's got to get rid of you. You following me?"

Nick nodded. "He brings up this business of me being a juvenile without a family and tries to have me committed to a home so I'll be out of the way."

"Exactly. Only Judge Murdock didn't go for it."

"He would have if you hadn't shown up."

"Maybe. Anyway, he left you here. Jessup has to be desperate for money. So he had to take the chance and go ahead with his midnight logging, hoping you wouldn't find anything. You wouldn't have if you and Connie hadn't gone looking for George."

"That proves Mr. McCumber's innocent," Nick said. He began to get excited. "Let's go tell Sheriff Perkins."

Idaho shook his head. "That's how it had to happen, but we can't prove one word of it yet."

"You mean Mr. McCumber stays in jail and Jessup gets away with this?" Nick asked angrily.

"That's right. Unless we can snare this old fox."

"How?"

"That's the tough question." Idaho stood up. "I'll think about it while we put a couple of logs in the river."

They worked almost two hours. Idaho said nothing, but his brown eyes were thoughtful. Finally, after the second log had been eased into the raft he asked, "How's this raft compare with the one you sent to the mill?"

"It's almost half again as big."

"Shut off the 'cat.' Let's talk."

They found a dry place under a tree and sat on the fir needles. "We can take it for granted," Idaho said, "that Jessup needs money to make machinery payments, a lot of money. If he can't raise the cash he'll lose the equipment and everything he's invested in it. If he'd already stolen enough logs to make the payment he wouldn't have been out here last night looking around in the rain. So he's got to steal more. I'm sure he took those logs before I came, figuring you wouldn't find the stumps, and if you did find them you wouldn't know what they meant. With me here maybe he doesn't feel so safe and has held off, hoping I'd leave. But I'm still here and now he's getting desperate. Time's working against him. If he waits much longer McCumber'll be home. That'll end all his chances and he'll go bust."

"You figure he plans to try it even with you here?"

"I'm not sure. But we've got to make it real easy for him to come in again. We've got to catch him in the act of stealing a tree to make a charge stick and to prove the sneaky trick he pulled on McCumber."

"How do we do that?"

"You and I disappear."

"You mean walk off and leave Connie and Mrs. McCumber?"

"I know it'll be hard. But we've got to do it."

"If you're the one he's worrying about why should I leave?"

"Jessup was in the judge's chambers that day," Idaho explained. "He saw how glad we were to see each other. You can bet he knows I'm out here almost every day. He knows we're pretty close. If I quit coming he's apt to ask himself 'why'. Remember, he's sly and he's breakin' the law, so he's particularly sensitive to everything that goes on around McCumbers. We don't want him getting suspicious for one second. With both of us gone it'll open the gate wide. He and Lew will feel safe to come in and do their midnight logging."

"If we disappear, where do we go? And how do we catch 'em?"

"We need a place to keep outa sight during the day. At night we'll sneak back here and lay for 'em. When they come we notify the sheriff and he catches them in the act."

"You think it'll work? Seems like a lot of hocus pocus to me."

"Sometimes you've got to use a little 'now-you-see-it-now-you-don't' magic to catch a slippery character like Jessup. Police do the same thing all the time. It's called a stake-out."

When Nick just kicked at the dirt and scowled Idaho asked, "You got a better idea?"

"I haven't any."

"It's the only chance I see to catch 'em, get Mr. McCumber outa jail and clear his name. That's the most important thing, isn't it?"

"I'll have to explain to Connie and her mother."

"That's out. Too much risk. Connie or her mother might give it away by saying something or by the way they acted. Remember, Jessup'll be watching and he doesn't miss much. Connie and her mother's reaction to our leaving has to be real. No acting like they're disappointed or hurt. They've got to be. Best thing is to leave a note telling them we're leaving for California, then sneak out. It'll seem logical for a pair of typical bums to leave that way."

"It'll sure make me out the bum Connie's always said I am," Nick said.

"That's how we want it."

"How long do you think it'll take to catch them?"

Idaho shrugged. "Who knows when they'll come, or if they'll even come? Remember this whole thing's built on the belief that they haven't got the money to make their payment—and that's assuming they have to make one. In fact we haven't any real proof it's the Jessups."

"Sure a lot of guessing," Nick said.

"Maybe. But it's the only logical explanation I can find to explain those hidden stumps, Jessup's efforts to commit you to a home, and his charge that Mr. McCumber stole a few of his second-grade logs."

"Where'll we hide?"

"I saw a deserted cabin when I was taking a hike along the river one day. I'll check it out again. I'd better leave early. I'll have to quit the mill, collect my money, buy us a couple of blankets and some grub, and look over that cabin."

"You want to start tonight? But I need a day or two. I've got to split firewood—and things," he said lamely.

"Do it this afternoon," Idaho said. "Time's important to us, too. We can't stall on this, partner. It'll be just as hard to leave tomorrow night as tonight."

"I suppose so." Nick fidgeted uncomfortably. "Sure don't like Mrs. McCumber thinking I'm a run-out kind of tramp."

"She'll know better when we catch 'em."

"If we catch 'em," Nick said.

"That's right. And we won't if we sit here gabbing about it. Let's get back. Meet me tonight at my boarding house soon as you can get away."

They returned to the house and Idaho took off for Jewel. Nick began splitting wood for the fireplace and piling it under the shed. Norah McCumber came out and asked where Idaho was.

"He had to go back to town," Nick said.

"I'd have taken him in."

"He didn't want to bother you."

Nick spent the afternoon splitting wood. When it was time for Ad Nelson to drive his cows past the house he cut through the timber and met him in the road. He asked Ad if he'd milk morning and night for a few days. "I've got to be gone," he explained. "I'll pay for milking."

Ad smiled. "Sure. But no pay. The McCumbers are friends. When do you want me to start?"

"Tomorrow morning."

"Fine," Ad said. "I'll take care of it."

Nick returned to the barn, put grain in the mangers, and let in the cows. George came in and walked straight up to Nick for his hand feeding of pellets. Nick dug half a dozen from his pocket. Then George went into his own small stanchion and Nick left him there for Connie to feed.

He was halfway through milking when Connie came in. She fed George, petted him a minute, then asked, "How about teaching me to milk. I could help."

"It's not bad," Nick said. "I'll finish soon."

For the first time Connie was in no hurry to leave. She watched and finally said, "Tim didn't say a word about last night. I'll bet he doesn't know."

"Probably not," Nick said. "George sure saved us from being caught."

"Good old George." Connie smiled. "He sure ran those two ragged. I'll bet Mr. Jessup's still mad."

"Bet he is." Nick finished milking and stood up. "Better make sure George doesn't go near Jessup's. Lew'll kill him sure."

"He'd better not," Connie said darkly. She added

then, "I kept wondering all day what Mr. Jessup and Lew were doing out there in the dark and the rain."

"I've no idea."

"They looked sort of sneaky," she said thoughtfully.

"Why don't you ask Tim? Maybe he knows."

"Oh, him." Connie waved a hand in dismissal. "All he's interested in is keeping that black, curly hair fluffed up and shiny."

"It looks nice."

"Oh, sure, if you like black, curly hair." Connie went off to gather eggs.

For some unaccountable reason Nick felt better than he had in days. Then he remembered he was leaving tonight and felt miserable.

All through supper he thought about the note he had to write and of leaving. Finally Norah McCumber asked, "Are you feeling all right, Nick?"

"Sure," he said. "Why?"

"You're so quiet."

"Nick's wondering what Lew and Mr. Jessup were doing out there last night," Connie said. "So'm I."

"There's never any telling what that old man's up to," Norah McCumber said.

Nick got a fire going in the fireplace, waited until Connie and her mother had settled down in the living room, then said he guessed he'd turn in early and went upstairs.

He stood at the window looking out at the night lying over the barn and sheds and the indistinct field beyond. Finally he found a piece of paper and pencil and composed a note to Norah McCumber. He said that Idaho was leaving for California and he was going with him. He explained that he'd split enough fireplace wood to last until Mr. McCumber came home. That Ad Nelson would milk night and morning. That the raft in the backwater was big enough to send to the sawmill. He hesitated over how to end it and finally wrote, "By the time you read this tomorrow morning I'll be a long way from here."

He laid the paper on the dresser where she couldn't help finding it. Then he sat on the bed and waited for the women to retire. He was glad he wouldn't be here to see Norah McCumber's face when she read the note, or to hear what she said.

Finally Connie's light steps came up the stairs. A few minutes later her mother passed his door. Nick gave them plenty of time to get into bed and settle down. Then carrying his shoes he went out and down the stairs. This time he avoided the treads that squeaked. He put on his shoes at the back porch, went down the steps, and walked into Connie. She was wearing a bathrobe and slippers.

Nick said the first thing that popped into his mind, "I thought you were in bed."

"I forgot to turn out the chicken lights. Where you going?"

The lie came instantly to his lips. Then he realized this was a perfect opportunity to make his leaving so logical no one could question it, so he said, "I'm leaving."

"What do you mean, leaving?"

"Pulling out, going away. Idaho's heading for California tonight. I'm going with him."

"But why, Nick? Why?" Connie's face was all twisted up with shock.

"Because I'm what you always said I was, a tramp, a bum. We never stay long in one place."

"I don't believe that. Not about you," she insisted. "There's some other reason."

"Sure," he said, "a whole flock of 'em. But one's enough. The minute your dad gets out that judge'll put me in some home. The day I came here I said they'd never do that. So I'm getting out."

"But, Nick, we don't want you to leave. I don't want you to leave."

"You ought to be tickled to death," he said brutally. "You can quit worrying about me sneaking into your room some night and cutting your throat."

"Nick, I'm sorry. I didn't really mean that. I didn't know you then." She reached for his hand.

Nick pulled away, "You don't know me now. You never will."

"Please, listen to me, Nick. Please." He saw the tears come suddenly. "I don't feel that way any more. Honest, Nick. Honest."

"I do," Nick said. "And don't waste time calling the sheriff. I'm an expert at dodging cops." With that he ran off into the night.

At the road he glanced back. He thought he saw her shadow still standing by the back steps looking after him. But he wasn't sure.

# 11

When Nick arrived Idaho was in his room. He had his coat and hat on. A blanket roll tied with rope lay on the bed. " 'Bout gave up on you," he said. "We're all set to go." He indicated the blanket roll. "Got enough grub in there to last us about a week, if we don't eat too heavy."

"What did the sheriff say when you told him?"

"Haven't told him yet. Been too busy. By the time I quit, drew my pay, got these blankets and grub, paid my landlady, turned in the key, and found us a place to stay the day was gone. Figured we'd go see him when we left here."

"Did you find a place?"

Idaho nodded, "The abandoned fisherman's cabin I told you about. It's right on the river bank but hidden from the river by brush. It's almost straight across the river from the McCumber property and a little upstream from the site where we've been loggin'. Even found an old rowboat there that we can repair and use to row across the river at night to stake out our watch."

"Is there a road to it?"

"No road. Walk up the railroad track and cross the river on the trestle. There's an old half-grown-over trail leading off to the left through the brush right to it. How'd you make out?"

Nick told him about writing the note and running into Connie as he was leaving. "After what I told her there's no question I'm the number-one tramp."

Idaho was suddenly in motion. He grabbed the bed roll, his voice urgent, "Let's get outa here fast. I've a feelin' we're about to be visited by Norah McCumber lookin' for you. Move, partner, move!"

They ran down the stairs and outside. The McCumbers' old car was just turning into the driveway. They ducked around a corner of the house. Norah McCumber and Connie got out and went to the door. They talked to the landlady a minute, then returned to the car. They were about to get in when a long, wailing whistle rode the stillness. Then came the hollow rumbling of a freight across the trestle. Both women listened until the sound was gone. "I hope Nick likes California as much as he thinks he will," Norah McCumber said. Then they both got into the car and drove away.

Idaho whispered, "That's fine. Just fine. Now let's see the sheriff."

Sheriff Perkins had a small office in his home where he could conduct business in the evening. He lounged in an old swivel chair behind the desk and grinned at Nick. "How's it going? Haven't had a chance to get out there. Norah tells me you're logging again."

"Everything's going fine," Nick said.

"Good, good. Now what can I do for you two this time of night?"

They both sat in straight-backed chairs before the desk. Idaho crossed his legs and said, "Discovered something this morning we thought might interest you."

"Okay, fire away," Perkins said.

Idaho told the whole story while Perkins sat frowning, turning a pencil in big fingers. When he finished Perkins said, "It's a pretty wild plan you've hatched and a far-fetched story."

"It makes sense. You know this logging business."

"Oh, it makes sense, all right. I've always found it hard to believe Frank McCumber would steal a few logs. I find it almost as hard to believe old Jessup would deliberately work out a plot to send a man to jail, then sneak in to steal logs. He's lived here all his life. He knows how serious that is."

"When your back's against the wall financially and you're about to lose big, sometimes you'll do things you wouldn't normally dream of."

"No question he's in a financial bind," Perkins agreed. "It's common knowledge he went head over heels in debt, then lost that contract because he tried to do a little extra chiseling on the deal. He hasn't made a dime with that equipment the past year." He tossed the pencil on the desk. "Maybe you're right. Certainly Jessup's capable of working out a stunt like this. He's pulled some pretty sharp ones in the past but he's always managed to stay just inside the law. This's way outside."

"Maybe he's never been in such deep trouble before."

"Could be. Let's say you're right. This scheme you and Nick have come up with to trap him is pretty far out."

"It's the only thing I think might work," Idaho said. "And it's no more off-beat than a regular police stake-out."

"You're not a police officer. And this whole maneuver hangs on a lot of assumptions, ifs, and maybes."

"Every stake-out does," Idaho pointed out.

"Have you given any thought to other alternatives?" Perkins asked.

"Like what?"

"Alerting mills and veneer plants to be on the lookout for Jessup's truck coming in with any big logs."

"Wouldn't prove a thing," Idaho said. "Once Jessup puts his brand on a log it's his. The only way we can prove where that log came from is to catch him before he takes it off McCumber's property."

"I guess you're right," Perkins agreed. "But I still don't like your scheme. It's just too iffy."

"Then you won't go along with it?" Idaho asked.

"I didn't say that. I just think the odds against you are awfully big."

"I know that," Idaho agreed. "But I believe it'll work—if I've figured everything out right."

Perkins held up a cautioning finger. "There's the catch. But I'll go along—with everything but one. Nick's out of it."

"Out? Why?"

"Judge Murdock released Nick to Norah McCumber, remember? And I'm supposed to look in on him every so often to make sure everything's going all right. That means I'm also responsible for him. And Murdock's a stickler. If Nick takes off, I'm in trouble and it puts Norah in a bad light."

"I'm not taking off," Nick protested. "It'll only look that way so we can lay this trap, make the stake-out."

"I understand that. But you do disappear, so it amounts to the same thing. Murdock expects me to make sure you stay at the McCumbers. And I don't dare tell him why you're not there."

"Why not?" Nick asked.

"He'd never go for it. I've known him for years and he's a very stiff-necked man. Why, he'd think I'd gone off my rocker for okaying this idea."

"If Nick goes back it'll cut our chances of success in half," Idaho said. "After what Nick told Connie tonight his coming back will seem mighty strange. We'll have to explain. Then they'll know. That's too many people in on it. Somebody could give it away."

"I see your point," Perkins admitted. "But it can't be helped."

"It might not be more than a day or two. You can wait that long."

"And it might be a week, or two weeks, or not at all," Perkins said.

"That's a chance we've got to take."

"That you can take. Not me."

"It's the only way we can clear Frank McCumber's name," Idaho said. "You thought of that?"

"I've thought of it." Perkins picked up the pencil again and turned it thoughtfully in his fingers. "Frank's a friend of mine. I'd like to try this your way. If I was reasonably sure this had a chance to work, even a fifty-fifty chance I'd take it. But the way I see this it's a long, slim shot. I can't go for it."

"I don't agree with you," Idaho said.

"It's what I think that counts. Judge Murdock won't consider it and I don't dare."

Nick had been listening and thinking. Now he said, "It seems like this whole thing depends on me one way or another. If I go back to the McCumbers like you insist, it practically gives the whole show away, and what chance we had to make it work becomes no chance at all. If I don't go back I'm in trouble with you and Judge Murdock. I figure I'm in trouble with Judge Murdock anyway. I won't get any better deal from him than I'd have got in Chicago. He wants me to hang around the McCumbers until Frank McCumber comes home, then he's going to ship me off to some home."

"I don't know that," Perkins said. "Neither do you."

"I know it all right," Nick said. "I tried to tell myself at first that out here it'd be different. You just set me straight."

"Don't go jumping to conclusions, Nick. You agreed to stay until Frank comes back."

"I agreed to stay. Not to be shipped off to some home. I'll never go for that."

Perkins lounged behind the desk completely relaxed. Nick could reach the door in two fast steps.

Perkins would have to come around the desk to reach him. Nick eased his chair back carefully and got his feet firmly under him. His muscles tensed. "When I left Chicago," he said, "I was headed for California. I still am." He looked at Idaho. "I'll see you. You know where. I'm cutting out!"

Nick was at the door in two strides and jerked it open. He'd forgotten it opened inward. That slowed him a fatal second.

Perkins lunged erect and started for him. "Nick!" his voice was sharp. "Nick, hold it!"

Perkins was quicker than he'd expected. The big man was around the desk, his long arm reaching for him before Nick got started through the door.

Sure-footed Idaho, who could sprint through loose railroad grade gravel, leap and never miss a traveling boxcar ladder, tangled awkwardly in his own feet and fell full length into the reaching Perkins. Both men sprawled on the floor. As Nick yanked the door shut he got one fleeting glimpse of Idaho's face looking up at him. One warm brown eye closed in a wink.

Nick raced down the walk, dodged behind a hedge, and dropped flat on the ground. A second later the sheriff and Idaho burst out the front door. They stopped and looked up and down the dark street.

"Not much chance findin' him now," Idaho said.

"Guess not. But I sure don't enjoy the prospects of trying to explain this to Judge Murdock." He scowled at Idaho. "Mighty funny you tripping right at that exact moment."

"It happened," Idaho said. "Just clumsy."

"Maybe," Perkins growled. "If I could prove what

I'm thinking I'd be tempted to toss you in jail. So help me."

"Why?" Idaho protested. "I didn't want Nick to take off any more than you did. I've been nursing him along for months. I feel responsible for the boy."

"Anyway, he's gone," Perkins said. "You think he'll really cut out for California?"

"That's all he's talked about since the first night I met him," Idaho said.

"Do you think he'll hop a freight? We could lay for him."

Idaho shook his head, "There's a dozen places he could get on and he might cross us up by hitching a ride. I taught him plenty of tricks. You'd never catch him."

"He said he'd meet you in California."

"We agreed on a place a long time ago in case we were ever separated."

The two men turned back toward the house. The sheriff asked, "You still figure to go ahead and try to trap Jessup?"

"I feel sorry for Mrs. McCumber," Idaho said. "But I guess you're right, the chances are pretty slim. Anyway, I don't see much sense going on with it now that Nick's gone."

Nick waited until they disappeared into the house, then hurried away.

# 12

Nick followed the railroad track upriver and crossed the dark trestle. He began looking for the half-grown-over trail in the dark. He finally found one and followed it until it ended on the river bank. But there was no cabin. Nick hunted along the bank for some distance then decided it was not the right trail. He returned to the railroad track and went on, keeping a sharp lookout for any break in the brush that resembled a trail.

He traveled almost a mile before he found another. It was clear enough leading down off the right of way, but then a mat of brush obscured it. Nick pushed through. A few feet farther on he made out the trail again leading off through a growth of small trees. He finally came out on the river bank in front of a one-room cabin. He looked across the river, and against the night sky made out the high, ragged shapes of trees that he guessed must be the Mc-

Cumber woods. He thought about going inside, then decided against it, sat down on the porch and waited for Idaho.

Nick had been there almost a half hour when Idaho came through the trees, the blanket pack slung over his shoulder. Nick rose and said, "I was beginning to wonder if you'd come."

"I couldn't walk right out and leave the sheriff after you did your busting-out act. I had to stick around and talk a few minutes so he wouldn't become suspicious. Perkins is nobody's fool. Maybe it's just as well he thinks we're both pulling out for California. Now nobody knows but you and me."

They went inside. Idaho struck a match and Nick saw the cabin was about twenty feet square. There was an old table, a couple of benches, and three wooden bunks. A stone fireplace took up one corner. There were pieces of kindling near the fireplace. Idaho found paper and built a small fire. In the dim light he untied the blanket pack, took out a dozen cans of food, and handed Nick a blanket. "This isn't too much bedding but we'll keep a fire going to drive off the chill. Pick yourself a bunk."

"You think this grub will last us?"

"Who knows. They might be in there right now cutting a tree. Then again it may be a week or more."

"The sheriff doesn't think they'll come at all."

"That's the chance we're taking," Idaho agreed. "I think they will. If we run out of grub I know a little out-of-the-way store where we can get supplies. In fact I'll slip up there in the morning and pick up a couple of loaves of bread."

Nick spread his blanket on a bunk and observed, "Perkins doesn't think much of our idea, does he?"

"It's a bit unusual, I admit. But sometimes you've got to use unusual ideas to catch a thief."

"I sure hope it works."

"Time'll tell," Idaho said.

"Suppose it doesn't work. Then what?"

"We won't think about that. Not yet. We have, in a manner of speakin', burned our bridges behind us. We've bet everything on this trick. All we can do now is sit back, wait, and hope. Let's turn in, it's getting late."

Nick could not sleep. He lay on the hard bunk and watched the flickering shadows on the ceiling. The fire finally died down. Darkness settled thick in the old cabin. He listened to the night sounds, the river lapped against the bank a few feet away. A night bird cried. A frog started up and announced that spring was coming. The more he thought about it the crazier this scheme seemed. But Idaho thought it was good. Idaho should know. That was his only hope. He finally slept.

Next morning Idaho went to the store early and brought back two loaves of bread. Then they got the old rowboat into the water. It hardly leaked at all.

"Now, that," Idaho said, "is something. Been lying in the weather all winter and the rain kept the cracks from opening up. She's not exactly a pleasure cruiser. But she'll take us across the river and bring us back. That's all we want."

They spent the remainder of the morning gathering wood for the fireplace. In the afternoon they lounged about waiting for night. Idaho took a nap, explaining to Nick, "We'll be up a good share of the night. You'd better get some sack time, too."

It was full dark when Idaho doused the fireplace fire and they set off. Idaho rowed. They crept out onto the black body of the river without a sound. It was the first time Nick had ever been on a river at night. The current was stronger than he'd expected. Idaho worked hard with the oars. There was a surprising amount of debris. A chunk of timber struck the side of the boat and pushed them partly around before it slid off and disappeared. A tree top went by. A stump loomed out of the darkness, roots upthrust like octopus tentacles. "Where'd all this stuff come from?" Nick asked. "I never saw any before."

"Spring's almost here. Snow's beginning to melt in the mountains. The run-off is bringing the river up. There'll be a lot of junk coming down. You'd better watch out for us. We could hit something big enough to swamp this old tub, and I can't swim."

A few minutes later they grounded on the mud bank of the opposite shore. They worked the boat under a screen of brush, tied it to a root, and took off through the trees. Within a hundred yards they came to the spot where they'd been logging. The raft was still in the backwater. It took only minutes to arrive at the little opening where the hidden stumps were.

Idaho chose a rotting log in the shadows of overhanging trees to hide behind.

They made themselves comfortable and Idaho explained, "If they come it'll likely be fairly early at night because it's a slow job to fell a tree with an old cross-cut, then buck it up, haul it out, and clean up the brush and limbs. As soon as they come and start work you slip off to the McCumbers and call the sheriff."

"What'll you be doing?"

"Watching them while you're gone."

"Suppose they leave before the sheriff gets here?"

"That's another chance we're taking. We've got to catch them in the act to prove this, remember. If the sheriff doesn't get here in time we'll have to wait and hope for another night. One thing, we've got to be quiet. They might not return to this spot. They might choose another and we've got to listen for any sound like a cross-cut saw or the muffled exhaust of a big motor."

Heavy mist began to fall. It became chilly, then wet. Moisture dripped from the trees and fell steadily into the grass and low brush. Somewhere a small animal scurried through the grass. An owl talked briefly from a tree. A pair of deer wandered into the small clearing, fed across it, and disappeared into the dark under the trees. Time dragged. Nick wanted to stand up and stretch his cramped legs and to ease cold muscles. But he didn't dare. He must have slept. The next he knew Idaho was shaking him and saying, "Come on, partner, we might as well call it a night."

Nick straightened up and rubbed his eyes. The heavy mist had stopped. Fog banners drifted through the trees. "What time is it?"

"Almost three o'clock."

"There's still a couple of hours before dawn."

"Not enough time to get a tree out and clean up

before it's light," Idaho said. "Besides, we don't want to be seen on this river."

Nick kept careful watch on the way back so they'd not hit some big object. At the cabin they built up the fire, opened a couple of cans, ate, and crawled into their bunks.

Such was the pattern of their days. They always hid the boat under the overhanging brush and passed their old logging site on the way to the hiding place. The raft Idaho and he had cut was still there.

They spent their nights behind the log. Twice they toured through the woods to make sure the Jessups were not logging somewhere else. They found nothing. "I didn't think so," Idaho said. "We'd have heard something."

"Maybe they've taken all the logs they need?"

"Or Jessup's being especially cautious."

Some nights it rained and they were miserable. Sometimes there'd be fog. They could scarcely see the opening and the near trees stood about like dim ghosts. Then again the sky was star-filled. The night was lighter and the black bulk of mountains rose over them edged by the ragged timber line. At such times Nick felt small and helpless and discouragement weighed him down. Some nights the silence was complete. On others the forest was alive with furtive scurryings and scratchings. The chill night breeze stirred the fir boughs. They groaned and sighed as if in anguish.

The river continued to rise. The water turned brown. The current increased. More debris was floating by, whole trees, logs, chunks of planks and timbers. Sometimes a section of wall from some old building bobbed along. Idaho always handled the oars. Nick watched and called out warnings.

Ducks and geese began passing over, heading north. Idaho would glance up and smile. One night a flock of geese splashed to rest in the river near them. Idaho stopped rowing and said, "Not long now. Not long." Nick caught a faint excitement in his voice he'd never heard before. Buds began swelling on the maple and cottonwoods. The ends of the fir tips turned gray and soft with the beginning of new growth. It was the first time Nick had ever watched spring come.

They ran out of food. Idaho hiked to the little out-of-the-way store for more. That night as they ate bread and beans Nick asked, "How much longer? It's been more than a week and there's been no sign. Nothing. Maybe we're wrong, and Jessup had nothing to do with it. It's somebody else. Or maybe they've taken all the logs they need and we're wasting our time."

"Could be we're wasting our time," Idaho agreed. "But your conclusions are only partly right. It has to be Jessup. He's the only one for miles around who has a Lumberjack. You could be right that he's already taken all the logs he needs."

"Then what do we do?"

"Nothing we can do. Like I told you when we started this, we've burned our bridges behind us."

"How much longer do we keep this up?"

"Do you want to quit?"

"Not as long as there's a chance. But I'm beginning

to think there isn't any. This is the seventh day."

"I'm not as sure as I was." Idaho frowned. "Something should have happened before now. But I'm not quite ready to call it off yet. Let's wait until we finish this new batch of grub, three or four more days. If nothing happens by then, we quit."

"Then what?"

"I've already been here longer than I usually stay in one place. I might as well pull out."

"For California?"

"Of course."

"I'm going with you."

"You thought any more about settling down here with the McCumbers?"

"That's impossible," Nick said.

"You're sure?"

Nick nodded, "If they'd wanted me they could have asked me to stay before Mr. McCumber went to jail. They didn't. They won't now."

"All right," Idaho said, "when the grub's gone so are we."

The days crawled by. The third evening they finished the grub. Idaho flattened an empty tin can and said, "Well, this's it. Can't say as I'm sorry it's over. I'm tired of eatin' outa tin cans."

Nick had an empty feeling at the thought of leaving. He said, "You don't figure to go over there tonight?"

"We said the end of the grub. Well, this's it. Did you wanna go over there once more?"

"The grub lasted three days," Nick said. "But we've only been over there two nights. This would make it three days of grub. Three nights of watching. Sort of even it up."

"All right," Idaho agreed. He shook his head thoughtfully. "Seems I figured this whole thing wrong. I'd have bet I was right."

Nick kept thinking about leaving as they rowed across the river for the last time. He was surprised that now the time had come how much he dreaded it. They were close to the opposite shore when disaster boomed out of the night. Nick was so engrossed in his own thoughts he hadn't been watching closely. When he became aware of the huge stump it was bearing down upon them. Thick roots were upthrust against the stars like grasping arms.

Nick yelled, "Idaho, look out!"

Idaho twisted his head. That moment the stump slammed into them. The oar broke with a snap. The boat twisted crazily. Huge roots slid across the top and held them fast. Idaho stood up, fighting to push the boat free. Nick scrambled forward to help. The bow went down, the stern shot skyward. Nick went flying through the air. He struck with a splash and the dark water closed over him.

Nick went deep. The icy current tumbled him over and over. He stroked wildly for the surface, his lungs screaming for air. When his head broke water the stump was thirty or forty feet off and drifting away. He could not see the rowboat. There was no sign of Idaho. Nick struck out for shore. He was not a particularly good swimmer and the coldness of the water seemed to freeze his muscles. The current swept him downstream.

He finally made the bank and climbed out. He was shaking with cold and near exhaustion. He searched the dark water for Idaho's bald head, or an arm thrown up out there. There was nothing. Far down the black bulk of the stump was fading into the night.

Nick ran along the bank following it, crashing through brush, scrambling over rocks and logs searching for some sight or sign of Idaho. He ran until he was out of breath and leaned against a rock to rest. Then he remembered Idaho couldn't swim. Idaho had drowned and it was his fault. If he'd been watching the way he should have been, instead of thinking of himself, he could have warned Idaho in time. Grief overwhelmed him. He put his head down against the rock and began to cry.

# 13

Nick didn't know how long he leaned against the rock wracked by grief. Gradually he became aware of an odd sound that he'd been hearing for several minutes. It was a steady, measured swish-swish that carried softly on the night's stillness. He listened, and knew what it was. This was what Idaho and he had waited for night after night. The excitement that should have picked him up lay dead within him. Idaho was gone. Nothing else mattered. He felt numb and cold, as if the coldness of the river had gotten inside him.

The sound continued. Finally he remembered there was still a job to do—his job. Idaho would want it finished. He wiped his eyes and drew a deep breath. He'd run out on Idaho once. Not this time. Resolutely he put any thoughts of Idaho from his mind and struck off through the trees in the direction of the sound.

It was closer than he thought. He came to the little

glade almost before he was aware of it. He crept forward to the down log and peered over. The swish-swish was so close and loud he could hear the sing of metal. It was a cloudless, starlit night. Every detail stood out. He recognized the two men. Old Man Jessup and Lew had felled a tree and cut off the limbs.

Now they stood on opposite sides of the log cutting it in two with a cross-cut saw. It looked like they were about a fourth the way through the first cut. There were at least two more big cuts in the log. Nearby was the black bulk of the Lumberjack, the huge machine with pincer-like claws that would carry the logs out of the woods. Idaho had guessed right. Good old Idaho!

Nick crept stealthily away. When he had a screen of trees between himself and the Jessups he ran.

At the house Nick didn't bother to knock. He burst through the door and rushed into the living room. Connie and her mother were there before the fireplace. Connie was studying. Norah McCumber was doing embroidery on a pillow case.

Connie jumped up and began to squeal, "Nick! Nick! You're back!"

Norah McCumber dropped the pillow case, "Why, Nick!" she said. "Why, Nick!"

Nick said in a rush, "I never left. Just listen and don't interrupt." Breathlessly he sketched the plot Jessup had used to put Mr. McCumber in jail and why.

"Then we can prove Dad's innocent," Connie burst out. "We can prove he didn't do a thing to old Jessup."

"Of course he didn't." Norah McCumber's eyes were shining. "But, Nick, how . . . .?"

Nick explained how Idaho and he had lain in wait night after night. "Call the sheriff," he finished. "Tell him to get out here fast. We've got to catch them in the act."

Norah McCumber was already at the phone. Nick waited while she called. When she turned her face was sober. "Cal's gone to Woodland. He'll return sometime tonight. His wife doesn't know when. Oh, Nick, what'll we do?"

"Stay on the phone. Keep trying," Nick said. "I'm going back up there."

"Suppose they finish before Cal comes?"

"I'll think of something," Nick said. "You just stay on the phone."

Connie started for a coat. "I'm going with you."

"You stay here. If Perkins comes he'll need you to show him where it is."

He was at the door when Connie asked, "Where's Idaho?"

"He—he drowned crossing the river tonight," Nick said. Then he slammed the door and ran.

In the yard George trotted up to him going "Mm-m-m-m," and looking for his handout of pellets. Nick shoved him aside and ran up the dirt road into the timber.

The Jessups were finishing the first cut when Nick crept to his hiding place behind the log. They began the second. It took about forty minutes. They stopped several times, twice to rest. Jessup complained that he wasn't as young as he used to be, and that he hadn't pulled a cross-cut in years. They stopped to oil the saw when it began to stick, and again for Lew to drive a wedge into the cut to hold it open. Nick watched, praying that Sheriff Perkins would come striding through the trees.

They had finished the cut when something touched Nick's arm and there stood George watching him expectantly. Nick's heart jumped into his throat. He shoved George away, whispering fiercely, "Get out of here. Go on, beat it. Beat it!" George came back, shaking his horns, front feet dancing as if to play. Any second he might let out a blatt. Nick grabbed him, pulled him close, and clamped a hand over his nose. Luckily the log was high enough so George's head didn't show. He struggled a little, but Nick held tight. Finally George stood quietly. The Jessups had begun the third and last cut. Once that was finished they'd get the logs out fast, clean up the brush, and be gone. And there would go any chance to clear Frank McCumber tonight. Nick's mind kept racing in the same old track. Perkins had to get here and catch them in the act. But with the passing of each minute it became more doubtful that the sheriff would arrive in time. He was still hoping for Perkins when it came to him that he didn't need the sheriff here. All that was necessary was proof a tree had been cut and that Jessup had done it. The Lumberjack standing there and the logs was all the proof anyone needed.

A cold ball settled in Nick's stomach. He had to get to that machine and do something so it wouldn't run. But what? If that motor was like an automobile engine it would have a distributor. In Chicago the kids easily knocked out a car motor by taking off the distributor cap and removing the rotor. Without that part, smaller than his thumb, no motor would start.

Nick crept back from the log dragging George with him. The goat turned stubborn, braced his legs, and refused to budge. Nick yanked and whispered angrily, "Come on, you. Come on." George refused to move. He let go of George, scrambled backward on all fours until he was deep enough in the trees, then rose to his feet. George was still by the log looking toward him curiously.

Nick circled around to the opposite side of the clearing, putting the machine between him and the Jessups. He stepped into the clearing and tiptoed to the side of the Lumberjack.

The sawing continued. Nick peeked around the machine to make sure all was well. George stood out in the open watching the Jessups sawing. Nick would have scuttled back to the protection of the trees but that moment Lew said, "Pa, look, there's that dumb goat of McCumber's again! Now what's he doin' up here?" The sawing stopped.

Nick dropped to the ground and crawled partially under the Lumberjack, behind one of the huge wheels. Lew came into sight carrying a stick. "You dumb goat," he growled, "I'm gonna scatter your brains all over this clearin'." He ran at George, the stick raised.

George danced out of range. He galloped around the clearing making a game of this. Lew pursued, passing within a few feet of Nick. They circled the machine a couple of times but Lew got no closer. Old

Man Jessup said finally, "Let'm go. He's just a goat. Can't do no harm. Let's finish this job."

Lew stopped, panting. He glared at George who had stopped and was looking back at him. Suddenly Lew swore and hurled the stick with all his strength. George bounced nimbly aside and trotted off. Lew went back to the saw muttering, "Always hated that goat. If I ever catch 'im . . ."

Nick waited until they began sawing again. Then he crawled from under the machine and began searching along the side of the motor. He found the spark plug wires and traced them down to the distributor cap. It took but seconds to unsnap the cap, remove the rotor, put it in his pocket, and replace the cap. Then he scuttled into the dark safety of the surrounding trees.

George was not in sight.

Nick watched them finish the cut. Lew crossed to the Lumberjack and climbed to the cab. He began grinding on the starter. The starter ground and ground. Lew fiddled with the levers. He choked the motor. Old Man Jessup came over and suggested, "Maybe you're outa gas."

"Can't be," Lew said. "I filled the tank before we left home. It's just plain dead. It don't make sense. When we came down here it was runnin' fine. Now it acts like it's not gettin' any spark."

"You're the mechanic," Jessup said.

Lew descended from the cab and began feeling about the motor. Nick plainly heard him snap the clamps off the distributor cap and held his breath. Next Lew lit a match and bent over studying something. "Pa!" His voice was surprised. "Look here!"

Old Man Jessup looked with him. "See that," Lew said, "that's the distributor. There's supposed to be a rotor on that post—and it's gone. Without a rotor we can't move this machine one inch."

"Go up to th' house and take one off th' 'cat' or a truck."

"They won't fit. But that ain't what's important, Pa. That rotor was on when we came down here."

"So it fell off."

"No way. The cap holds it on. I just took the cap off." Lew peered around the darkness. "Somethin' fishy's goin' on here."

"You startin' that again," his father said annoyed. "You've been jumpier than a grasshopper in a hot skillet ever since we started. Relax."

"Pa, you don't get it. Somebody had to take this cap off, reach inside and take that rotor out, then reclamp the cap in place again. Somebody did that while we were workin'."

That moment George minced into the clearing again. "McCumber's goat! It ain't natural him being up here this time of night alone. And on this night especially. He came up here with whoever took that rotor out." Nick saw the shine of the long, slender knife blade. "Maybe that kid stayin' with the McCumbers didn't go to California after all."

Old Man Jessup picked up a club. "I guess we'd better look around." They started moving in Nick's direction.

Nick began tiptoeing away. He never knew if he made some small noise George heard, or the goat knew where he was, or his sharp eyes spotted Nick. But George trotted toward him shaking his head and going "Mm-m-m-m."

Lew saw him and yelled, "Pa, here!" He came plunging through the brush.

Nick raced away. He hunted the thickest brush, the deepest dark under the trees to try to lose Lew. But Lew was lean and long-legged. He had known these woods all his life. No matter how Nick dodged and twisted he could not shake Lew. After a number of sharp turns Nick found himself on the lip of the river bank. He fled along it heading for the McCumbers. If he could reach the house Lew wouldn't dare follow. He came to the steep spot where he'd rolled logs into the river. Old Man Jessup loomed suddenly out of the brush in front of him. Apparently Jessup had followed the sounds of running and had taken a shortcut to head him off.

Nick turned sharply to dodge Jessup. He slipped and rolled down the steep bank to the water's edge. When he scrambled up Lew and his father were charging down the bank at him. There was no place to go but out on the raft. He leaped to the logs and started running across them.

Jessup called anxiously, "Boy, hold up. Wait. Wait. Let's talk."

Halfway out on the raft Nick stopped. Lew was about to jump to the raft when Jessup said sharply, "Lew, hold up. Let me talk to th' boy. You hear me, Lew? Come back here."

Lew stopped. He still had the knife in his hand. "Pa," he said, "he's seen us. We can't have that."

"I'll handle this," Jessup said, "leave be, Lew. Leave be."

"But, Pa . . ."

"I said I'd handle it. Now back off." Jessup stepped onto the logs and moved toward Nick. He was smiling, using his friendliest "good neighbor" voice, "Now listen, boy. We don't wanna do nothin' foolish, do we? We can settle this with no trouble to anybody. All we want is that little rotor thing you took off the machine. That's positively all. Nothin' more. So why don't you hand it over and you can go. Better yet, they tell me you wanna get to California. I'll see you get there, boy. First class, too. How about that?"

Nick began backing along the log. "I haven't any rotor."

"Why, sure you have. Right in your pocket." Jessup moved carefully in his smooth-soled rubber boots. He held out a hand, "Why don't you give it to me and get shed of it? There's nothin' in this for you but trouble."

George minced out of the shadows and came down the bank. He stopped at the water's edge and looked toward Nick.

Lew was so intent watching Nick and his father he didn't see the goat.

Jessup kept edging forward talking in his most persuasive voice. "We don't aim to hurt you, boy. But we've got to have that rotor. No two ways about it. So you'd better give it to me before we have to take it."

Nick pulled the rotor from his pocket and drew back his arm. "One more step," he warned, "and I'll throw it."

"Boy," Jessup's voice was suddenly ugly, "you wouldn't dare!" He lunged at Nick.

Nick hurled the rotor far out into the river and jumped to the next log. Jessup's boots hit a slick spot. The next instant his feet flew from under him and he crashed flat on his back. The club shot from his hands and wedged between two logs.

Jessup got shakily to hands and knees. The next instant Lew yelled, "Pa, look out!"

Jessup, on all fours, was more temptation than George could resist. He had leaped to the logs, and head down was charging full tilt with a goat's surefootedness, straight at the old man. He struck like a hundred-pound projectile. With a startled yell Jessup was driven head first over the end of the log into the river.

Jessup came up sputtering, got his hands on the end of the log, and began to pull himself out of the water. Lew jumped to the raft and ran forward. Nick grabbed the club the old man had dropped and brought it down on his fingers. Jessup yelled and fell back into the river.

George stood on the log in Lew's path shaking his horns. Lew aimed a tremendous kick. George hopped nimbly to the next log and trotted calmly ashore.

Lew came at Nick, crouched slightly, the knife extended as if he meant to use it. Nick swung up the club and waited. He heard Jessup thrashing about. He was trapped between the advancing Lew and the old man crawling out of the river behind him. He wanted to rap Jessup's fingers again and drive him down. But he didn't dare take his eyes off Lew.

A figure ran down the bank and jumped lightly to

the logs. Almost as if he were dreaming Nick saw the dull shine of the familiar bald head, the swing of wide, thick shoulders. He almost shouted his surprise and pleasure.

Idaho was halfway out when Lew heard his steps and whirled. Nick saw his lunge, the knife shoot toward Idaho's middle. He didn't know what happened next but Lew went sailing through the air with a startled yell. He hit the dark water and went under.

Nick remembered Jessup and brought the club down on his fingers. Jessup went back into the water and Nick stood there, club raised ready to hammer him again.

Lew's head bobbed up. Idaho yanked him out of the river, twisted his arm behind his back, and held him as easily as he would a child. He grinned at Nick. "You'd better let that old man out of the water before he drowns, partner."

Nick let Jessup crawl laboriously on top of the raft. His overalls were plastered to his gaunt frame. He'd lost one boot and his hat. His white hair streamed water. He was shivering and he held his right hand with his left and scowled at Nick. "Wasn't no cause to smash my hand, boy," he said through chattering teeth. "No cause at all."

They herded the two men ashore and Nick said, "I looked and looked for you. I thought you'd drowned."

"I grabbed a root of the stump when the boat went under," Idaho said. "The current finally set the stump ashore about two miles downriver. You and George were having a right lively time when I got here."

Nick looked around. George had disappeared again.

They had reached the top of the bank when Nick heard Connie yell, "Nick! Nick! We're here!" A powerful light beam cut the night and Sheriff Perkins, Norah McCumber, and Connie arrived.

Perkins said, "Rather odd place to find you this time of night, Mr. Jessup." He took out handcuffs and linked Lew and his father together.

"You can't do this," Jessup sputtered. "You got no right."

"I think we can find a right. Norah tells me there's a little hoot owl logging going on here. Mind showing me where, Nick?"

"Now, Cal," Jessup said in his heartiest "good neighbor" voice, "there's no need for traipsin' around these woods in th' middle of th' night. If you'll take these cuffs off we'll forget all about this little misunderstandin'."

"We'll take the cuffs off after we look," Perkins said. "Lead off, Nick."

Nick led the little cavalcade through the trees to the clearing. Perkins flashed his light across cut logs, saw, ax and wedges, the big Lumberjack. Nick told them what he'd done to the machine.

Norah McCumber kept murmuring, "I can't believe it! I can't believe it!"

Connie kept staring at Nick, her eyes big and round.

"Now, Cal," Jessup blustered, "don't go jumpin' to conclusions."

"Am I jumping to conclusions?" Perkins asked.

"I'm tellin' you, it ain't what you're thinkin'."

"What am I thinking, Mr. Jessup?"

"You're wrong, Cal, dead wrong. I'm a respectable, law-abidin' citizen. Laws don't look kindly on handcuffin' a citizen. You know that, Cal."

"It looks less kindly on log stealing," Perkins said. "Of course there's a logical explanation for what I see here."

"Sure there is. Sure." Words tumbled out in Jessup's hurry. "I can explain everything. It's all a mistake. A big mistake. I can explain."

"I wish you would."

"Uh, well." Jessup rubbed a hand across his mouth. He rolled his tongue in his cheek as if he wished he had a chew. "Well, you see. . . ."

"Take all the time you want," Perkins said.

"It's like this, Cal. Uh . . ."

"Pa," Lew burst out. "It won't work. It just won't work. I told you it wouldn't. I told you, Pa!"

Old Henry Jessup looked at his son, then at Norah McCumber and Sheriff Perkins. Then his eyes took in the cut logs, the tools, the big Lumberjack. He shook his head hopelessly. His shoulders sagged. He said miserably, "We was about to lose it all, machinery, money. Everything. What else could I do? What else?"

He didn't look clever, or sly, or dangerous to Nick. He was just a beaten, discouraged old man who'd been caught stealing.

# 14

Cal Perkins brought Frank McCumber home in the police car late the next afternoon. He got out lean, smiling, and healthy looking. He was immediately set upon by Connie and her mother. It was bedlam for a few minutes with everyone crying, laughing, and firing questions no one answered. Nick and Idaho and Perkins waited for the first excitement to pass.

Finally Frank McCumber shook hands with Idaho and told him how much he appreciated all he'd done. He put an arm around Nick's shoulders, his gray eyes bright. "I knew you could take care of the place. I didn't guess you could do all the rest. Nick, I'll be in your debt as long as I live."

Sheriff Perkins filled them in on everything that had happened since last night. Lew and his father were in jail. Lew was scared and talking his head off. Old Henry Jessup had made a full confession. It was exactly as Idaho had figured. "The old man's broke,"

Perkins said. "He's going to lose all the machinery, the money he's got in it, and go to jail for railroading Frank. Also for log stealing, if Frank wants to push it."

Frank McCumber shook his head. "I'll take the money for the logs he took and make sure my name's cleared. Otherwise let him go."

"What about Tim?" Connie asked. "Did he know what his father and brother were doing?"

"No. They worked at night when Tim was asleep. Jessup didn't want Tim to know for fear he might let something slip. He's going to send Tim to live with an aunt in another state." As he was leaving Perkins said to Nick, "Judge Murdock will want to settle your case in a few days, I suppose."

"I guess so," Nick said.

After Perkins had gone Nick said, "There's a raft in the backwater. It can go to the mill anytime."

Frank McCumber smiled. "Thanks to you and Idaho the McCumbers didn't go in the hole one penny while I was gone."

"What will you do now?" Idaho asked.

"Keep on logging."

"You should be cutting that big peeler stuff."

"That takes a big 'cat.' I can't afford one yet."

"I've been thinkin' about that," Idaho said. "Jessup's going to lose his machinery. His 'cat's' a good one and it's big enough. I'll bet you can get it from the company for ten thousand and your old 'cat.'

"I don't have ten thousand."

"I'll loan you the money."

"You'll what!" Frank McCumber looked startled.

"I'll loan you the money," Idaho repeated. "I've

looked over your timber. It's choice. And I like the way you're going at this business."

"Idaho," Frank McCumber laughed, "we're talking about ten thousand dollars."

"I'll take the regular bank rate of interest," Idaho said.

"You mean it," Frank McCumber said surprised. "Where'd you get ten thousand dollars?"

Connie piped up, "Idaho's not a tramp or a bum, Dad. He's a real knight-of-the-road."

"I didn't mean that," Frank McCumber said quickly. "It's just that, that . . . Well, maybe I did," he finished. "How did you accumulate that much when you ramble around the country all the time?"

"Let's say I'm a businessman with no particular office and who doesn't keep office hours." Idaho smiled. "Now, about that loan."

"You know nothing about me, Idaho."

"I know quite a bit."

"Take his word for it, Frank," Norah McCumber said smiling.

"All right. What about security?" McCumber asked.

"The 'cat's' security."

Bells began ringing out on the road. Nick glanced out the window. Ad Nelson was driving his cows past. George came mincing up the lane. It was time to let in their own cows.

Nick slipped out, let the waiting Fawn and Blackie into the barn, and fed them. George followed Nick about looking for his usual handout. Nick fed him a handful of pellets. Then he put George in his small stall and returned to the house.

was gone.

went back to town," Norah McCumber ex-
ed happily. "He's going to lend us the money to
Jessup's big 'cat' as soon as it's repossessed."

'Did he say when he was coming out again?"

"No."

Later Frank McCumber and Nick did the chores together. The man said, "Sure good being back doing this. Didn't know how much I missed it." They were returning to the house when he added, "I'm glad you moved out of the shed."

After supper Connie and her mother wanted to hear all about the weeks on the jail farm. The fireplace was lit and they sat together on the couch while he talked. They seemed to be conscious of nothing but each other.

Nick listened awhile then left the room. "Where you going?" Connie asked.

"I'll turn out the cows and George."

Nick put on his hat and coat and went outside. It was a bright night. The stars were out. The moon rode high over the timber tops. He turned the cows out. Then he got another handful of pellets, turned George loose, and hand fed him, smiling at the soft, velvety touch of his lips. "You're sure an ugly brute," Nick said, patting the hard head. "I wouldn't trust you as far as I could throw you. But I love you anyway. You might have saved my life last night when you belted old Jessup into the river." George finished the pellets, then minced outside to inspect a near bush.

Nick stood in the barn doorway and looked at the house. He heard the sleepy complaining of the chickens. There was spring softness in the breeze that touched his cheek. Of all the places he'd been with Idaho this was the one he didn't want to leave.

He knew Idaho meant to catch a freight out tonight. He hadn't said good-bye to Nick because he was giving him every chance to stay here. He didn't know how impossible that was. After watching the three McCumbers on the couch talking, laughing together as if there was no one else in the world, Nick did know. They were a family. They didn't need or want anyone else.

Nick closed the barn door, cut diagonally through the trees, and came into the road below the house. He began to hurry.

Idaho was sitting beneath the trestle, his back against one of the trestle legs. Nick sat down near him.

Idaho looked at him. "Nice night for travelin'."

"Yes," Nick said.

Idaho moved his shoulders for a little more comfort. "Those McCumbers are mighty nice people."

"Yes."

"Girl's nice, too."

"Yes."

"Reminds me a lot of that place I told you I almost stayed once. Should have stayed. Trouble is a man's hindsight's always so good. I was pretty young. Didn't think as straight as I should. Funny thing, when it's too late you know what you should have done. Then you can't call back one single solitary second."

"Sometimes you don't have a choice," Nick said.

"That happens. But you've got to be sure you've

looked at it from every angle: that you haven't jumped to a wrong conclusion."

"I know," Nick said.

Idaho was silent. He looked at the sky, then off across the dark canyon. He adjusted his shoulders again. Finally he said, "You'll like California."

"I figure to."

Idaho looked up at the dark lacework of the trestle. "Ought to be along in a few minutes."

"Yes," Nick said.

They had lapsed into silence when feet scrambled down the bank and Frank McCumber's tall shape came under the trestle. He squatted on his heels and looked from one to the other. "You fellows left kind of sudden like. There's a couple of things I'd like to say to both of you before you go. I owe you money. Nick, for taking care of the place, logging all those weeks. You, Idaho, for helping him."

"You owe me nothing," Idaho said. "I was giving my partner a hand. I had nothin' else to do."

Nick said, "I stayed because I wanted to. I don't want pay for that."

"You're hard men to do business with," Frank McCumber said.

"Let's go up on the tracks," Idaho suggested. "Our private car's due in a few minutes."

They climbed to the tracks and Frank McCumber said to Nick, "We want you to stay, all of us do. How about becoming part of the McCumber clan? I'd have asked you sooner but I wanted to talk to the women."

Nick thought of them sitting on the couch wrapped up in each other and shook his head. "I don't belong."

"Don't belong? You took over running a two hundred acre timber tract, logged six hundred dollars' worth of timber alone, took care of a couple of women, animals, helped trap the people who were stealing logs, and cleared my good name. How much do you think it takes to belong?"

"I don't know."

"Not that much I can tell you. Nick, Norah and I lost a son and Connie lost a brother. We'd like you to take his place."

"Judge Murdock won't go for it."

"Yes, he will. I talked with him this morning after Cal came up to the farm and got me."

"Connie doesn't go for bums and tramps."

"Connie's learned some things. Why, you and Idaho are not only knights-of-the-road, you're all decked out in shining armor to her. Go ask her. She's right over there in the car waiting with her mother. You should have heard the howl she put up when she learned you'd left. You got any other objections?"

"No."

"Then how about it?"

"I'd like it," Nick said. Then he glanced at Idaho and felt torn up.

"I know," Frank McCumber said. "You'd miss Idaho and he'd miss you. I said I wanted to talk to both of you." He turned to Idaho. "We agreed on a loan to buy Jessup's 'cat.' How about staying and becoming a part of this? There's plenty of timber for three of us to work as a team. Besides, Nick'll be in school part of the year and that'd leave you and me. The McCumbers would be mighty happy to have you."

"Why, now," Idaho said surprised, "that's a real generous offer. It truly is."

"It's great," Nick said. "It's perfect."

"I never expected anything like this," Idaho said. "I don't hardly know what to say."

"Say yes," Nick said happily.

"It's mighty sudden," Idaho said. "I've got to think about it a little."

"You always told me there was no percentage in ramming around the country all your life," Nick reminded him.

"I know," Idaho said.

"A man should settle down, put down roots."

"Of course."

"Become part of a community, have a home, friends."

"That's right."

"There's more to living than watching the world go by an open boxcar door. Remember that?"

Idaho smiled. "I surely do."

"Then it's settled. You'll do it?"

Idaho scuffed a toe thoughtfully in the gravel, then looked up at Frank McCumber and said soberly, "Of all the places I've been I've only found one I liked as much as yours. I thank you for the offer. I really do." Then he stopped and tipped his head up, listening.

In the soft dark Nick heard the sound. It came from high overhead, filtering down through deep layers of silence, adding magic and mystery to the night. Nick looked up and saw the black V of a great flight of geese moving majestically against the star-studded sky, winging their way north as they'd done for countless centuries. Their happy gabbling filled the night. Idaho watched until they were lost to sight.

He was still smiling when he looked at Nick and Frank McCumber. To Nick there was sadness in the smile and a kind of eagerness that had seemed to be in the voices of the geese.

Idaho shook his head. "It'd never work. For a few weeks, a month or so it'd be fine. But I've been beating the rods too many years, partner. I'd begin itching to know what was around the next bend, over the next hill, what exciting wonderful thing I was missing staying in one place."

"You told me that wonderful thing doesn't happen."

"Maybe not today," Idaho said. "But there's tomorrow."

Nick wanted to go on arguing. But he didn't. He asked instead, "Will you stop by in the fall?"

"Every fall and spring. You can depend on it."

A light beam probed the night. The freight rumbled onto the trestle. They watched it come. Nick caught himself automatically searching the passing cars for an open door. He found it the same moment Idaho did.

Idaho squeezed his shoulder, "Be seein' you, partner. Good luck." He was gone, running lightly through the dark. Nick saw him reach the door and heave himself inside. He wanted to call out a farewell but his throat was dry. His eyes stung.

They watched the freight fade into the night. Finally even the sound was gone. Frank McCumber dropped an arm over Nick's shoulder and they walked toward the waiting car.

WALT MOREY is the author of many well-known adventure stories for young people. RUN FAR, RUN FAST was drawn from Mr. Morey's own youth. The Angora goat, George, was modeled after his own pet, Billy. He was born in Hoquiam, Washington, an old-time logging town where his father was a logger. As he says, "I was practically born with sawdust in my veins. . . . And as for riding the rails I've done enough to know what it was like and how to do it."

Mr. Morey and his wife live outside Portland, Oregon.